THE FREEDOM TRILOGY:
Book I

DON PENDLETON'S

THE EXECUTIONER®

─ FEATURING ─

MACK BOLAN®

**A brutal dictator
fans the fires of war
in Eastern Europe**

D0027629

BATTLE
PLAN

GOLD EAGLE · 61174 · $3.50

ISBN 0-373-61174-9

9 780373 611744

50350

1 58030

The room erupted into chaos

Mack Bolan threw himself to the floor, covering the First Lady as another burst of gunfire added to the confusion. The warrior reached under his jacket for the Desert Eagle, his eyes probing the curtain of smoke.

A South Haakovian soldier aimed his subgun at the warrior, who focused on the man's emotionless face. He'd seen it many times before, in the terrorist files at Stony Man Farm—Dag Vaino.

More billowing smoke enveloped the terrorist, and he disappeared in the thick gray cloud.

Bolan leaped to his feet. "Stay here!" he ordered Varkaus, then sprinted into the hall after Vaino. He knew that if he didn't take out the terrorist before he escaped from the castle, the man would disappear into the throngs of people gathered on the grounds.

The warrior took the stairs two at a time. Reaching the landing, he raced around the corner and continued down.

He spotted the near-invisible wire a split second too late. The mine exploded from a doorway to Bolan's right, the concussion throwing him into the air.

MACK BOLAN®

The Executioner

DON PENDLETON'S

THE EXECUTIONER®

FEATURING

MACK BOLAN®

BATTLE PLAN

A GOLD EAGLE BOOK FROM

WORLDWIDE®

TORONTO • NEW YORK • LONDON
AMSTERDAM • PARIS • SYDNEY • HAMBURG
STOCKHOLM • ATHENS • TOKYO • MILAN
MADRID • WARSAW • BUDAPEST • AUCKLAND

First edition June 1993

ISBN 0-373-61174-9

Special thanks and acknowledgment to
Jerry VanCook for his contribution to this work.

BATTLE PLAN

Printed in U.S.A.

...it is not for glory, nor riches, nor honour that we fight, but for Freedom only, which no good man lays down but with his life.

—Declaration of Arbroath,
1320

Freedom is never voluntarily given by the oppressor; it must be demanded by the oppressed.

—Martin Luther King, Jr.,
1964

The Wall has come down. It's time for all tinpot dictators to realize that people want the freedom to choose their own destinies. Whatever the repercussions, I'll do my part to aid the struggle.

—Mack Bolan

To those who would lay down their lives for freedom

PROLOGUE

Her hands trembled, and her mouth felt as if someone had rubbed sandpaper across her tongue. The lead weight that had dwelt in her chest since the war made her want to fall from the chair and curl into a fetal position.

Janyte Varkaus squinted beneath the bright overhead lights, then glanced nervously off-set to the bank of television cameras set up along the wall.

She had learned to live with stress over the past few months. What bothered her far more than shaky hands and a dry mouth was the new feeling that encompassed her, a cold chill of outright terror that shot up her spine every few seconds.

It didn't feel like stress.

It felt more like imminent danger.

Janyte turned back to the set. Her eyes tried to focus on Amy Bray, who was seated across from her. The dark-haired newswoman fired another question at Janyte's husband, but the woman's lips seemed to move in slow motion.

"President Varkaus," Bray said, her face now frozen in the hard-yet-feminine smile that had become her trademark, "rumor has it that President Stensvik has sent assassins from North Haakovia to kill you. Would you care to comment?"

Janyte glanced to her side in time to see her husband's gray eyebrows rise in amusement. "Why does no one want to take our situation seriously?" Edvaard Varkaus asked. "It is not *rumor*, Ms. Bray. South Haakovian intelligence sources, as well as those of the United States, have confirmed the assassination order as fact."

Bray nodded. "That explains the tightened security around the castle."

Janyte's eyes moved to the squad of armed South Haakovian military guards that ringed the set, then turned back to the bank of cameras, one of which moved in for a close-up. She studied the new crow's-feet around her eyes, then turned away from the lens.

She looked bad, and it would do neither her husband nor the people of South Haakovia any good to see the stress she was under. Still watching the screen from the corner of her eye, Janyte forced a smile.

"We live in a state of constant threat," Varkaus said. "There was war. For the moment there is peace. We do not know when the hostility will break out again—only that it will. North Haakovia is the last Communist holdout in the Baltics. It has become a haven for some of the worst fiends Marxism ever produced, and President Franzen Stensvik is the worst of the worst. He is intent on reuniting Haakovia. Well, so am I. But under democracy, not communism."

"You are certain North Haakovia will resume the fighting?" the newswoman asked.

"Stensvik possesses weapons of mass destruction that were stored north of the river before the Soviet Union dissolved," Varkaus replied. "And when he believes the time is right he will not hesitate to use them."

Janyte continued to watch the monitors. Suddenly another cold chill shot up her spine. She stiffened in her seat, squinting, not believing what her eyes told her brain they'd just seen on the screen.

Was a rifle scope really transposed over her husband's forehead? She glanced at him.

The South Haakovian president continued to talk to Bray.

Janyte looked back at the screen. The rifle scope was gone. She let out a long sigh of relief. She had imagined it.

The comfort was short-lived. Her relief gave way to another surge of terror as she realized the rifle scope must have been a hallucination. Now she was seeing things. How far away could the nervous breakdown her doctor feared be?

The first lady of Haakovia shifted in her seat and crossed her legs. No. She would *not* break down. She couldn't afford to do so, especially on television, in front of the entire world. She forced her eyes back to the screen, concentrating, forcing her breath to remain even as she confronted her demon head-on.

Yes, she thought, her eyes were simply playing a few tricks on her. It was just another symptom of the stress she was under.

Janyte Varkaus gasped out loud as the rifle-scope cross hair reappeared. Her mouth fell open and she gaped at the screen. Then a gunshot exploded, echoing against the stone walls of the castle.

Frozen in her chair, her gaze still locked on to the television monitor, Janyte watched her husband's head burst apart.

The picture disappeared from the screen and was replaced by the leering face of Franzen Stensvik. The North Haakovian dictator wore a brown N.H. army uniform festooned with gold general's stars and brocade. His piggish eyelids fell to half-mast, and he glared through the slits. Then the lids rose high to reveal the eyes of a madman.

Stensvik spoke into the camera, the scraggly mustache on his upper lip bounding in time to his words. "The American puppet state of South Haakovia will no longer be allowed to keep our country divided." Stensvik paused, then his voice rose as he proclaimed, "We will bury you!"

Janyte stared transfixed at the demonic face. Distantly, as if in another life, another dimension, she heard more gunshots. Smoke filled her nostrils, and she felt heat against her cheek as something flew past.

Her chair was struck from behind, and suddenly she found herself on her back on the floor. She blinked, then looked up to see the hard face of Rance Pollock.

"Stay down!" he yelled.

Janyte started to nod, but before she could do so, another shot rang out and she felt the weight of the big man fall protectively over her.

Chaos ruled.

Explosions sounded around the set. Voices screamed, smoke rose in the air and pistols and machine guns chattered with deafening intensity.

Mack Bolan, a.k.a. Colonel Rance Pollock, dived forward, driving his shoulder into the back of Janyte Varkaus's chair. A rung cracked and the woman shot forward to the floor as he scrambled over her on hands and knees.

"Stay down!" Bolan ordered, then shielded her body with his own as the bullets continued to fly.

The voice of Franzen Stensvik droned on in the background. "We have learned from the mistakes of our comrades in North Korea and Vietnam. We will never allow..."

Bolan rose slightly, squinting through the smoke, his eyes burning. The warrior registered movement to the side.

One of the guards was raising his pistol.

Bolan leaned down again, covering the first lady as another loud crack echoed through the confusion. His hand searched beneath his sport jacket for the .44 Magnum Desert Eagle as his eyes probed the smoke.

The guard prepared to fire again.

The Executioner's eyes focused on the deadpan face above the South Haakovian uniform. He had seen it many times before, in the terrorist files at Stony Man Farm.

Dag Vaino.

More smoke bombs erupted around the terrorist and he disappeared in the thick gray cloud.

Bolan leaped to his feet. "Stay there!" he ordered Janyte Varkaus, then sprinted after Vaino. Screams of terror pierced the pandemonium. Through the clamor, the Executioner's battle-trained ears heard running footsteps, hurrying toward the door to the hall.

The warrior followed, his index finger moving away from the trigger to the guard. He couldn't shoot blindly through the haze—the smoke hid the innocent as well as the guilty. He'd have to wait, identify his target, before he squeezed the trigger.

A sudden blast of fire speared through the smoke. Bolan heard the discharge and felt the pressure as a bullet whizzed past his left ear. He dived toward the muzzle-flash, hitting the ground on his shoulder, as three more rounds blew over his head.

The footsteps were louder now. Bolan got to his feet, angling through the cloudy wall where the door should be. Somewhere ahead he heard a click. A light flashed briefly as the door opened, then disappeared. He headed toward the light, misjudged and felt the cold jagged edges of the castle's ancient stone walls.

The Executioner let the fingers of his free hand walk him to the door, the Desert Eagle held at chest-level. In one smooth motion he jerked the knob and dived into the hall.

As he'd known they would, more rounds flew over his head.

Bolan rolled to his belly in time to see Vaino's emotionless face. The terrorist fired another round, then turned and fled around a corner at the end of the hall.

As the Executioner got to his feet and sprinted after his prey, the terrorist's intel file flashed through his mind. *Vaino, Dagmar Hugo. Finnish by birth, Marxist by choice. Master espionage agent and terrorist. Specialization: Sniper/Assassin.*

The warrior remembered the words stamped in red at the bottom of Vaino's Stony Man Farm spec sheet: Extremely intelligent, Skilled and Dangerous.

Bolan reached the end of the hall and rounded the corner, crouching in case Vaino waited in ambush. He saw a dead South Haakovian soldier sprawled out next to the wall, then more rounds flew past him like a swarm of bees. He fell forward, his shoulder striking something soft and furry in the semidarkness. He returned fire, rolling over the body of one of the South Haakovian army's German shepherd attack dogs. Blood oozed from the bullet hole in the animal's head.

The Executioner jumped back to his feet. Again he heard the tapping of footsteps somewhere ahead. More shots sounded. He turned another corner and saw the bodies of three more fallen S.H. troops.

Bolan knew that Vaino was no fool—he planned his escapes with the same careful strategy as his sniper attacks. And he always used a backup team.

So where was the team?

Bolan found out.

A man wearing black fatigues and a stocking cap leaped through a doorway off the hall. An Uzi submachine gun hung from the sling over his shoulder. The barrel rose.

The warrior pumped two rounds from the Desert Eagle into the man's gut and raced on.

Three more specters in black crowded into the hallway. The Executioner emptied the Desert Eagle into the first two as his left hand drew the Beretta 93-R from shoulder leather. A 3-round burst punched into the chest of the final attacker, taking him down and out.

Bolan encountered no more resistance and suddenly found himself at the top of a stone staircase in the ancient Viking castle. He slowed to a walk, letting the Beretta lead the way and keeping his gaze locked on the steps to the second floor as he descended.

Below, an arm shot into the stairwell from the side. A wild shot snapped up and over the Executioner's shoulder.

Bolan threw himself back against the stone wall. As the echo died, he heard Vaino's footsteps descend to the ground floor.

The warrior took the stairs two at a time. Reaching the landing, he sprinted around the corner and continued downward. He knew Vaino hadn't intended the snap shot to kill him, just slow him down, give the assassin a few more vital seconds to lengthen his lead.

Bolan pushed on, fully aware that if he didn't catch Vaino before the terrorist left the castle, the man would disappear into the throngs of people that had gathered outside. Fire shot through his lungs as he gasped for air. First his calves, then his thighs began to burn as lactic acid built up in the flexing muscles.

He spotted the almost invisible thread a split second too late.

The trip wire had been set waist-high to make sure he didn't pass over it. It snapped like the tape above the finish line of a footrace as the Executioner sprinted through.

Cause and effect raced through his mind in a microsecond. Bolan knew the bomb itself would be set a few yards farther down the halls, timed to put him in the nucleus of the explosion as he kept running.

He also knew there was no way he could stop in time to avoid it.

Leaving his feet, the Executioner vaulted into the air, straining toward the ceiling and pulling his knees to his chest.

The mine exploded beneath him from a doorway to his right. Shrapnel blew across the hallway, several smaller pieces rising high enough to shred through the back of his thighs and calves. The concussion drove him higher, then forward as multicolored lights flashed through his brain.

Bolan's head struck the stone floor as he fell back to the ground. He gasped for air as his body settled in the debris.

Shots rang out around him. Blinded, the Executioner rolled across the cold stones. His mind still spoke to him, ordering him to keep moving, not to give the enemy a stationary target. He jerked to his left, then reversed direction as the gunner anticipated his move. Turning toward the roar, his vision began to clear, and he saw Dag Vaino standing near a side exit to the garden.

The bore in the end of Vaino's pistol stared the Executioner in the eye.

Bolan raised the Beretta and pulled the trigger. Vaino fired simultaneously. The Executioner's round sailed over the assassin's shoulder.

Vaino ducked, then charged through the door. Still dressed in the South Haakovian army uniform, he saluted the guards at the gate as he passed through and disappeared into the crowd.

RETRACING HIS STEPS up the stairs of the castle, Bolan's strength began to return as the aftermath of the concussion wore off. His injuries weren't serious, nothing a little disinfectant and a few bandages wouldn't take care of. He silently cursed the fates that had favored Dag Vaino.

Nearing the third floor, the warrior heard voices and quickened his step. He passed the three corpses in black fatigues and came to the prostrate form of the first man he'd shot. Several South Haakovian soldiers stood over the dying man. A young private looked up at his sergeant as Bolan approached, then back to the body.

"He is alive, Sergeant Erikson," the private said in English.

The sergeant unsnapped the flap on his holster and drew his gun. He glanced at Bolan, nodded, then aimed at the terrorist. "We shall correct that immediately." He pulled back the pistol's slide and chambered a round. The hard metallic click echoed eerily down the stone hallway.

Bolan stopped next to them. "No."

The sergeant looked up, his face puzzled. "But—"

The Executioner placed a hand on the forearm holding the gun. "Get him an ambulance," he said sharply.

"But Colonel Pollock—"

"Do it *now*. He might have valuable information."

The sergeant nodded, then turned to the private. "You heard the colonel," he barked. "Do it!"

Bolan knelt next to the terrorist. The man lay on his back, his eyes closed, gasping for air. Each labored breath shot a jet of crimson from the .44-caliber holes in his abdomen, but none of the rounds had struck a vital organ. Some of the blood had shot up over his face, but beneath the red, the Executioner could see the flat nose and almond eyes.

The man was Oriental, possibly one of the former Japanese Red Army members now reputed to be working for Stensvik.

Bolan studied the blood on the floor. The terrorist would need transfusions, but if the bleeding didn't kill him before he reached the hospital, he still had a chance of making it.

And telling the Executioner where Dag Vaino might pop up next.

The warrior opened one of the man's eyes with a thumb and forefinger. "Can you hear me?"

A low grunt escaped the terrorist's lips.

Bolan threw back the tail of his sport coat and unsheathed the Pentagon boot dagger clipped to his belt.

The terrorist's other eye opened on its own, then both widened as the blade came into view.

"You want to live, I imagine," the Executioner said.

Another grunt.

Bolan grabbed the tail of the man's black battledress uniform and sliced it into strips. "Okay. Help's on the way." He paused. "But it's not free."

He pressed a strip of cloth against one of the wounds and the man groaned in pain. "Here's the rules. I ask the questions. You answer. And you tell the truth. That's the price you pay for your life. Understand?"

The head nodded.

"What's your name?"

"Ta...da...shi...." the terrorist breathed.

Bolan put cloth over another wound, slowing the blood flow. "Were you hired by Vaino, Tadashi?"

The head nodded again.

The Executioner folded another strip into a patch. "Vaino's working for Stensvik, right?"

Affirmative.

"Where will Vaino go from here?"

Tadashi closed his eyes.

Bolan dropped the folded cloth on the man's chest and stood. "Okay, Tadashi," he said. "You don't want to play the game, that's fine by me. The medics ought to be here in another five minutes or so. But of course the way you're bleeding, you'll be dead by then." He turned to walk away.

Frantic grunts sounded behind him. He turned back.

"Where's Vaino going?" he repeated.

The lips beneath the terrified eyes moved unintelligibly. Bolan knelt again and leaned closer. Tadashi mumbled something, then passed out.

Down the hall, gears ground in the wall and then a bell chimed. The elevator door slid open, and two men in white jumped out. One man carried an oxygen tank, the other a folded stretcher, which he opened as they jogged down the hall.

The Executioner helped the medics load the dying terrorist and followed them back to the elevator as an oxygen mask was placed over Tadashi's face. He gasped for air, his eyes still closed.

Bolan looked at the medic next to him. "English?" he asked.

The man nodded.

"Will he make it?"

The medic shrugged. "It will depend on how quickly we get him to the hospital. We will start transfusions in the ambulance on the way."

The elevator doors opened on the ground floor. The Executioner helped the two men carry the stretcher out the nearest exit and through the garden to a protected parking area within the castle walls. Climbing in after Tadashi, he watched the medic start the transfusion.

Tadashi's eyes struggled open. The Executioner leaned in close to the terrorist's ear. "Where will Vaino go?"

Slowly the Oriental shook his head.

"How many men in your team?"

Tadashi held up all five bloody fingers of his right hand. Then his fist closed, and he held up three more.

"Eight. That include Vaino?"

Tadashi nodded.

The engine roared to life, and the ambulance started out of the parking lot. "Where's your operation base?" the Executioner asked.

Tadashi raised a hand to the oxygen mask. The fingers closed around the plastic, then the weak arm fell back to his side. His eyes closed again.

Bolan steadied the man as the ambulance pulled away from the castle and turned onto the street. As the red and blue lights atop the vehicle began to flash, he pulled the mask from the terrorist's face and held it to the side. Tadashi opened his eyes and gasped for air.

"Where do you base out of?" Bolan repeated.

"Near... Sturegorsk."

The Executioner held the mask back over the man's nose. Sturegorsk. The North Haakovian capital. Sturegorsk was also one of the many Soviet nuclear sites the North had taken over since the fall of the Soviet Union.

"The men under Vaino," Bolan said. "How many, total?" He removed the mask.

Tadashi shook his head in fear, the movement bringing pain to his eyes.

The ambulance slowed for another corner, then the driver hit the gas again as they pulled onto a broad four-lane street.

Bolan let Tadashi breathe a few minutes as they raced on. He knew he was walking a thin line. Too much exertion at this point could kill the Oriental. On the other hand, Tadashi stood a good chance of checking out anyway, and if Bolan didn't question him now, he might not get another chance. "You're Japanese," the Executioner said as he removed the mask again. "Where do the rest of Vaino's men come from?"

Tadashi coughed and his face contorted again. "Every...where," he breathed. "Former KGB... East...Germany, Poland, Czech...slav..."

Bolan replaced the oxygen mask. Like Varkaus had told Amy Bray, North Haakovia had become the last safe refuge for hard-core Communists. North Haakovian President Franzen Stensvik had fallen heir to more than just the nuclear sites, chemical arsenals, ground gear and a vast number of conventional weapons that were stored in the northernmost Baltic country.

Stensvik had gotten the cream of the crop of communist spies and terrorists, as well.

"What's Vaino got planned next?" Bolan asked. He moved the mask away.

Tadashi shook his head.

Bolan studied the man's frightened eyes. The Japanese was lying. The Executioner dropped the mask to the side. "Then there's no point in worrying about you any longer. You've told me all you know."

Tadashi's head jerked back and forth. He struggled to speak, but the words wouldn't come.

Bolan lifted the mask and placed it back over his face.

"Fin...land," the terrorist said immediately when the mask came off again.

Bolan frowned. "For what? What's he going to do?"

Tadashi's eyes closed. Bolan gave him another few breaths, then asked again. "What's he got planned in Finland?"

"Don't know...for..."

The Executioner placed the mask over Tadashi's nose and mouth as the ambulance slowed between the hospital and a two-story library building on the other side of the street. The driver turned into the parking lot and headed toward the emergency-department doors.

Bolan steadied the stretcher as they rocked over a speed bump. Finland had taken a strong stance against their neighbor to the south, fighting Stensvik's troops along the border and supporting South Haakovia with weapons and military advisers before the U.S. stepped in. Stensvik sending Vaino and his men to Finland made sense.

But to do what?

The shot came without warning. Bolan hit the floorboards as the rear windshield shattered. Thousands of tiny shards rained over his head and shoulders like a storm of glistening sleet. The Desert Eagle filled his hand as a second round was fired, and he felt its heat as it sailed over his head and through the back of the front seat.

The medic riding shotgun slumped forward.

The Executioner raised his head. Across the street he saw the man on the roof of the library. He'd changed out of the South Haakovian army uniform, but Dag Vaino's silhouette was still unmistakable against the clear blue sky as the terrorist held the rifle over his head and cut loose with a war whoop.

Bolan brought up the Desert Eagle in a two-handed grip and extended the barrel through the shattered windshield. But as the sights found their mark, Vaino dropped below the short concrete wall circling the roof.

The warrior lowered his weapon. There was little point in pursuing the assassin. Vaino was a pro. As he'd done at the castle, he would have mapped out his escape before climbing to the roof, and would be long gone by the time Bolan even crossed the street.

The warrior looked down at the man on the stretcher. Vaino's first high-velocity round had found its mark, drilling through the oxygen mask and into Tadashi's face.

Bolan stepped out of the vehicle. He stared briefly at the empty rooftop, then turned back to the dead man in the ambulance as three jeeps full of S.H. soldiers screeched to a halt in the parking lot.

The Executioner took a good look at the ragtag amateur soldiers who leaped from the vehicles. He had spent the past few weeks trying to whip them into a viable force that could withstand Stensvik's next attack. They were progressing, but they had a war coming and still had a long way to go.

Which meant that no matter how much he might like to pursue Vaino himself, he couldn't just desert them and head for Finland.

Bolan holstered the Desert Eagle and turned back to the library, a grim, determined smile flickering across his face. "No, Vaino," he said under his breath. "I don't have time to come after you myself."

The Executioner nodded slowly toward the rooftop. "But I know some guys who do."

IN THE OVAL OFFICE the President of the United States tapped the desktop with a pencil as he waited for the call to go through. The red plastic phone against his ear felt cold, distant, unfeeling.

Like the man with whom he was about to speak.

Besides placing the vast Soviet arsenal in the hands of unknown factors, the fall of the Soviet Union had meant the downfall of Mikhail Cheptsov. The warm working relationship the President of the United States had enjoyed with his Soviet counterpart had vanished into history. Dubious, enigmatic affiliations with the leaders of each of the new countries had taken its place, and the Man couldn't help wondering if the world was headed for another cold war.

Or hot one.

The President gave his old friend one final thought before returning to the problem at hand. It was ironic, really. Mikhail Cheptsov, the man who had started the wheels of freedom rolling in Eastern Europe and the Soviet Union, had been the first head to fall on the chopping block. He wouldn't be remembered as the first leader of a free Russia. Instead Mikhail Cheptsov would be written into the history books as the last oppressor of the Communist regime.

The President opened and closed a fist as he waited. The question now was how Niklai Tachek, the hero of the failed coup and new Russian president, had reacted to the new developments just north of Saint Petersburg. For some time now Tachek had been engaged in his own struggle to stay in office, and with Moscow breadlines practically backed up to the Black Sea, he'd had little time to worry about the Haakovian situation. But what scared the U.S. President even more were the mood swings for which Tachek was becoming internationally known. This man of peasant background was unpredictable, reacting rationally one day, reactionarily the next, and demonstrating surprisingly limited foresight as to the consequences of his actions.

That suggested a frighteningly conceivable scenario to the man in the White House.

If Tachek got too worried about the stability of his own position, he just might decide a good war could return his credibility. Russia would be backed by Ukraine and other former Soviet countries, which meant Stensvik would be defeated.

Which in turn meant the crazed president of North Haakovia might well resort to his nuclear arsenal.

The President's musings were broken by a click on the other end of the line. "Hello, Mr. President," the gravelly voice said.

"And hello, Mr. President to *you*," the Man returned.

A deep chuckle reverberated over the line from the other side of the world. The President frowned, trying to read it, trying to determine Niklai Tachek's temperament. Surely the Russian had guessed the reason for the call. Was his humor genuine, or affected for some other purpose? The President cleared his throat. "Perilous times we find ourselves in again, Mr. Tachek."

"I have known nothing else since I took office," the Russian leader replied. "It is simply more apparent these days."

"Yes." The Man paused, then said, "Janyte Varkaus has been voted into the South Haakovian presidency by an emergency session of parliament. I assume she will continue her husband's line of politics?"

"Our intelligence reports lead us to believe so," Tachek said. "We do not foresee any new problems from her." It was his turn now to pause. "Stensvik is the problem. I realize that, and for the part the Soviet Union played by allowing the weapons to fall into his hands, I apologize.'' He paused again, then said, ''Although I take no responsibility for it personally.''

''Do you have any influence over Stensvik?''

The chuckle on the other end of the line became a scoff. ''Stensvik is a madman,'' Tachek said.

Sweat broke out on the Man's face. ''I worry that if war erupts again it could spread, Mr. Tachek. We must move carefully, slowly. Stensvik is the most pressing problem either of our countries face. We must not act hastily—''

''Perhaps he is the most pressing problem *your* country faces, Mr. President. But *our* most dangerous threat comes from food shortages and the violence erupting in the streets around us.'' Tachek sighed. ''And while I agree with you about Stensvik personally, Mr. President, I cannot openly side with you. As you know, Russia's international telephone relay systems are located in North Haakovia. To do anything that might prompt Stensvik to cut them off would be political suicide for me.''

''He won't do that, sir,'' the President said quickly. ''North Haakovia is seeking a seat in the United Nations. Stensvik needs public approval. He's already denying he had anything to do with Varkaus's death. He must appear willing to cooperate with your government.''

''Let us both hope you are correct,'' Tachek replied. ''And let us also hope that applies to the nuclear sites under his control.''

The President sucked in air. "I don't know him, Mr. Tachek. You do. Tell me, in a worst-case situation, if North Haakovia fails to gain its UN seat, if they lose the war with the South...would he launch the nukes?"

Tachek remained silent for several seconds, then finally said, "Stensvik has a vision, Mr. President. He still clings to a doxology most of us gave up as quixotic long ago. And he is an animal. Shrewd and cunning like a fox, but with the viciousness of a shark and the survival instincts of a snake. His goal is to reunite the Baltic States and Eastern Europe under communism, then go after the rest of the world. Until he sees no hope of realizing his dream, he will never destroy himself."

"But what if all hope *is* lost at some point?" the President pressed.

"Then yes, I fear he is capable of self-destruction. Like the little monkey who eats all the bananas his belly will hold, then ruins the rest so no one else can have any. Or as you Americans like to say, 'He would cut off his nose to spite his face.'"

The President lifted a pencil from his desktop. Gripping it in his fingers, he said, "So we're damned if we do, damned if we don't. If he isn't stopped, he will take South Haakovia and then move into Finland or the other Baltic nations, gaining strength and power along the way. What will you do when he points his army toward Moscow, Mr. Tachek?"

The Russian leader didn't answer.

The pencil in the President's hand snapped in two. "So what will be your official position, sir?"

Tachek sighed again. "For now I will continue to look the other way concerning the American military 'advisers' in South Haakovia. But if civil war erupts again, I will have no choice but to publicly condemn the United States for impeding the reunification of Haakovia. And if it appears that the fighting may lapse over to Russian soil, or there is disruption of the Russian phone system . . ." He let his words trail off.

"What?" the American President pressed. "Finish. What will you do?"

"We will enter the war with whatever force it takes to protect ourselves. And on the side of whomever it appears will help us the most."

EIGHTY MILES BY AIR from Washington D.C., in the shadows of Stony Man Mountain in Shenandoah National Park, Stony Man Farm appears to be nothing more than a working farm. A landing field sits in the northeast corner of the property, hardly an unusual feature for a large twentieth-century agrobusiness. The crews in the fields explain the two-story outbuildings that flank the main house, for workers must have someplace to sleep. The large structure just south of the house is obviously a tractor barn.

From the outside, the main house leads the casual observer to the conclusion that the proprietor is a wealthy man cut from the same mold as the plantation owners who occupied Virginia's cotton land a hundred years earlier.

Security, both human and electronic, is state-of-the-art at Stony Man Farm. But if the ten-million-to-one long shot did come through, and some lost straggler accidentally found himself inside the house, he still might not realize that cultivation is only a secondary occupation. In the basement he would see nothing more deadly than power generators, as the gun and emergency-ration storage areas are hidden between the offices. The second floor would prove equally misleading, as it consists primarily of bedrooms and baths.

Stony Man Farm's secrets lie on the first and third floors.

The third story of the main house—better known as the Defense Level—is ringed with recessed windows made of bulletproof glass and steel. Here, assuming he would recognize them for what they were, the wandering stranger would see armor-plated garrets and realize that the large roomy area was really more fort than farmhouse.

Dropping to the ground floor, where most of the action takes place, our straggler would encounter quarters for the house staff, the kitchen and dining areas, a garage and shop. Here, too, he would see the Farm's security headquarters. On all but the rarest of days, he would find Stony Man Farm's mission controller, Barbara Price, busy at her console in the communications room. And a simple glance through the glass divider wall between comm and the computer room would give our curious friend a look at Aaron Kurtzman. Seated in his wheelchair at the top of the ramp leading to his computer bank, the man known as

"The Bear" would likely be wearing a rumpled lab coat and a frown of concentration.

The main armory can also be found on the ground floor. And if by now our straggler hadn't realized he had stumbled upon the headquarters of the most highly trained counterterrorist units in the world, the thousands upon thousands of weapons within the main armory would erase any lingering doubts that Stony Man Farm was only a farm.

As THE SUN ROSE over Stony Man Mountain and a cock crowed somewhere on the Farm, ten men and one woman took their seats around the large conference table in the communications room. Aaron Kurtzman guided his wheelchair to the control panel against the wall and pushed a button. Instantly the Oval Office appeared on the large television screen set in the wall, and the President of the United States smiled somberly into the camera. "Good morning, lady and gentlemen."

Kurtzman and the others returned the greeting.

"Will Striker be linked to us as well?" the President asked.

Hal Brognola, Stony Man's director of sensitive operations, liaison to the President, and high-ranking official within the Department of Justice, answered. "We've had a bit of technical difficulty, Mr. President," he said. He turned to Kurtzman.

"Bear, you about ready?"

Kurtzman had wheeled himself across the room to another large screen that faced that of the President.

He leaned forward, fiddling with the knobs on the panel below it. He nodded, said, "There," and pushed another button.

Mack Bolan materialized on the screen.

"Good afternoon, Mr. President," he said. "But I guess over there it's still morning."

The Man chuckled politely. "Yes." He looked into the camera and said, "Hal, why don't you take charge? I'll jump in if I need to, but you know this situation better than anyone."

Brognola straightened in his seat and dropped the half-chewed cigar in his hand into an ashtray. "Thank you, sir." He shuffled through a stack of computer printouts in front of him, laid one to the side, then began. "First, it goes without saying that we all know the struggle between North and South Haakovia isn't over. The war *will* begin again. We just don't know when." He took a deep breath, then continued. "I think a brief review of this divided country and its leaders might be beneficial. As most of you know already, Haakovia is the northernmost of the Baltic Republics. It borders Finland to the north. Saint Petersburg lies a few miles to the south. The Gulf of Finland is to the west, Lake Ladoga to the east. Originally settled by the Vikings, Finland took it away from them toward the end of the eleventh century. The Finns lost it under duress in 1939, when the land below the Inge River—presently South Haakovia—was ceded to the Soviets. What's now known as North Haakovia followed in 1944, going over to the Soviets as part of the armistice.'' He paused to sip from the coffee cup in front of him.

"Now," Brognola went on, "Franzen Stensvik. As the new Russian leader so colorfully described him earlier today, Stensvik is a madman, pure and simple. He grew up in the sticks of northern Haakovia, almost totally isolated from civilization. The son of an illiterate fisherman, Stensvik himself had no formal education before being drafted into the Soviet army. Due to his limited scope, he took to the socialist ideology hook, line and sinker. Stensvik reminds me of guys like Idi Amin and Manuel Noriega. He's not smart, but he's shrewd. Cunning. He's without principle, and like so many third world demagogues, he rose to power pretty much by just being in the right place at the right time. He's kept that power through fear, torture and brutality.''

Brognola shuffled through the papers. "Stensvik's military career was unremarkable, so I'll skip to the time of the Soviet coup. Stensvik deserted during the riots and returned to the area of his birth. During the next few months of confusion in the Baltics, he found himself leading a band of brigands that raped and plundered its way through Haakovia, Latvia and Lithuania.'' The Justice man looked up, glanced around the table and then to both screens. "Former Communist soldiers, intelligence agents and terrorists who'd escaped their fallen governments heard about Stensvik and headed to safety north of the Inge River. Stensvik's army of cutthroats grew until they outnumbered the Haakovian regulars. He seized control of Soviet military sites, which led to war with Edvaard Varkaus's regime and the division of the country. Stensvik then established himself as president of the North, but Varkaus retained power in the South."

Brognola glanced up from his papers to the President, then said, "He'd have taken over all of Haakovia if we hadn't stepped in."

The President nodded.

"Okay," Brognola said. "Let's get into the worldwide political aspects of what's going on." He turned to the tall, slender woman seated next to him. "Barbara?"

Price flipped open a manila file folder. "I'll briefly summarize, as well. At Varkaus's request, we have now sent close to thirty thousand troops into South Haakovia. Officially they're advisers. Our troops, and the bulk of the S.H. army, are amassed along the Inge River. Several Green Beret units, under the direction of Colonel Rance Pollock, are providing security and advanced training for select Haakovian troops and are based in Larsborg." She glanced up briefly, then returned to her notes. "Here are the various reactions from around the world in a nutshell. The Russians don't want to get involved. Their international telephone relay system is based in North Haakovia, and they don't want Stensvik cutting the lines. If they get forced into the situation, we have every reason to believe they'll support Stensvik. Finland poses resistance to Stensvik along the northern border, but they wouldn't last long under a direct attack. They've refused to allow U.S. troops on their soil, and cling to the mistaken belief that their borders are impenetrable."

Price looked up from her notes. "As we all know, the Hagakure Corporation in Japan began oil exploration in the South during the Gulf War. They found large deposits, and set up a billion-dollar industry that has set the standard of living in the South as one of the highest in the world. This is what Stensvik is really after, here. He's bullet rich but money poor, a situation that's reversed in the South. Since the war, the Japanese have been buddy-buddy with Stensvik in case he wins, and we suspect it's their money keeping his country afloat. They're still in business with Varkaus, of course, playing both ends against the middle."

A short man, older than the others and having an old-world air about him, interjected. "Can you tell us anything about where our own allies stand?" asked Yakov Katzenelenbogen, the leader of Stony Man's Phoenix Force counterterrorist team. "Can we expect any help from them?"

Price shook her head. "Britain, France and Germany are straddling the fence, letting us take the lead and waiting to see what happens."

Carl Lyons, the tall muscular ex-cop in charge of Able Team, spoke up. "So what else is new?"

Brognola frowned his way.

Price covered a smile. "The rest is pretty much what you'd expect. The remaining hard-line Communist countries—Vietnam, Cuba, North Korea—they're all backing Stensvik, not militarily yet, but certainly in his bid for recognition in the United Nations. We don't know why, but Colombia has joined them in negotiations at the UN."

"South Haakovia's already a member, right?" Hermann "Gadgets" Schwarz of Able Team asked.

Price nodded. "Officially it's just Haakovia, as the North has never been recognized. The South's diplomats are lobbying against the North. I understand it's come close to blows several times at the General Assembly."

"Where's Red China in all this?" Rosario Blancanales, Able Team's third member wanted to know.

"They're trying to deal with Stensvik but don't trust him. They'd love to have a beachhead somewhere in Haakovia so they could establish a pincer against Russia if it ever comes to that. They'd also like back the mineral land they lost after World War II. But like Japan, they've been hedging their bets, keeping an open line of communication to Varkaus. We assume that will remain the same with his wife."

The President spoke up. "Yes, let's never forget the monetary aspects of this whole thing. *Everybody* wants the South's oil."

Price nodded, then said, "That's all I've got."

"Thank you." Brognola turned to the screen across from the President. "Striker," he said, "sum up the military situation if you would."

"Right now we're at a standoff. But the clock is ticking, and it's ticking fast. Stensvik sent assassins, including Dag Vaino, into Finland, and Edvaard Varkaus's death proved what Vaino is capable of doing. The North has twenty tanks to every one of ours. Superior man and firepower on the ground and in the air." He paused. "And they've got nuclear weapons."

The President cut in. "Striker, I'd like to get your opinion on that. Would Stensvik really launch nuclear missiles if push came to shove?"

Bolan didn't hesitate. "Yes, sir, he would."

The room fell silent.

The warrior went on. "As for our side over here, we've got a ragtag army that I've been trying to whip into shape. But they're no match for the North, and they won't be, at least not in time to stop the inevitable. The bottom line, Hal, Mr. President, is that the only thing that's saved South Haakovia so far is the threat that the U.S. might enter this situation with guns blazing."

"And as we've already discussed, we're limited as to how far we can go," the President added.

Bolan shrugged. "Stensvik will figure that out soon enough."

"Hal," the President said, "give me a plan of attack. What can we do?"

Brognola pulled a sheet of paper from the bottom of the stack. "Without sending in the cavalry, here's the best I could come up with." He looked up at Bolan. "Striker, keep up the training and do the best you can with what you've got. Keep Janyte Varkaus safe, and design whatever covert actions you feel are necessary." He paused and drew a breath. "Do what you do best. You're on your own."

He turned to Katzenelenbogen. "Katz, your boys are going after Vaino in Finland. Remember, Helsinki not only didn't request you, they don't want you. So you're on your own without backup. First thing, I want you to infiltrate the country to show the Finns it can be done. Then locate Vaino and his terrorists."

Katz nodded. "And?"

Brognola glanced toward the President's screen, then back to the Phoenix Force leader. His face grew hard. "I don't think I have to spell it out for you."

Turning to Carl Lyons, he said, "Able Team, I want you to run down some of the leads on Stensvik's worldwide connections. He's got links to—"

The President broke in. "Just a minute, Hal. I'm getting all kinds of heat from the South Haakovians. There might be an assassination attempt on their delegates at the UN."

Brognola nodded. "Precisely why I've assigned our top Secret Service agents—"

The President shook his head. "I want Able Team running that show."

All heads in the room turned to the screen.

"Mr. President," Brognola said, "with all due respect, the Secret Service is more than capable of protecting the delegates. We'll set them up in a guarded room. They can broadcast their speeches over—"

"They don't want a guarded room," the Man replied. "They feel that won't be as persuasive as actually being there in the General Assembly."

Lyons straightened in his seat. "Mr. President, there's no way the Secret Service, Able Team, or the

Heavenly Host led by Michael the Archangel can guarantee their safety if they're allowed to run free." He glanced at Brognola, coughed, then looked back at the screen. "With all due respect, sir."

The President sighed. "I'm in a crack, gentlemen. There's no other choice. Do your best."

Brognola glanced at Lyons again, then shrugged. "Then Able Team will take charge of security at the UN. Handle it however you want to, Ironman, but make sure neither side, North or South, gets blown away." He stood. "People," he said, "we've got three parts to our objective if we're to prevent disaster, not only in the Baltics, but potentially for the entire world. We've got to neutralize the nuclear threat in North Haakovia. We've got to take out the cells of hard-line Communists hiding up there or else their ugly heads will pop up again down the line." He stopped and drained his coffee cup.

"What's the third objective?" the President asked.

Brognola looked up at the other screen.

"Execute Stensvik," the Executioner replied.

2

Ten miles east of Larsborg, the runways of South Haakovia's Erebure Air Base hummed with activity. American Lockheed Starfighters and McDonnell Douglas Phantoms dodged British Aerospace Harriers and Hawks, taxiing down the runways, disappearing into the skies, then returning to practice touch-and-go maneuvers.

Bolan pressed the field phone tighter against his ear. "Okay, Sergeant. We've already established that General Markus isn't in his office. What I said was, where is he?"

The man on the other end of the line coughed nervously. "Sir, as I stated earlier, I have no authorization to disclose—"

"Let's try this again from the beginning," Bolan said patiently. "This is Colonel Rance Pollock. You know who I am, and you know that authorizes me to—"

"Sir, I have no way of verifying your identity over the phone. If you'd care to come back to the general's office where I could check—"

A quartet of A-4 Skyhawks flying in formation overhead blocked out the rest of the words.

Bolan replaced the field phone back on the hook and turned to Jack Grimaldi, the crackerjack Stony Man pilot who had flown him on countless missions over the years. Grimaldi had spent the past few weeks trying to whip the South Haakovian air force into shape, and was about to take a brief recess from those duties to fly him into enemy territory.

If the equipment the Executioner had ordered from General Markus, the commander of all South Haakovian military forces, ever arrived.

Grimaldi raised his wrist and looked at his watch. "We're running out of time, Striker. It won't take long to get you across the river, but if you expect to hoof it into Sturegorsk and get your business done before the sun comes up—"

Bolan held up a hand and nodded. "I know, Jack. Everything else on board?"

Grimaldi jerked his head over his shoulder toward the F-14 Tomcat. "Everything except the long-range camera lens."

Bolan stripped the black ballistic nylon face-cover away from his own watch and stared at the hands. "Okay. Give it another ten minutes. Then we go, with it or without it."

The Stony Man pilot nodded.

The Executioner walked to the other side of the Tomcat and leaned back against the cockpit. He stared down the gravel road that led away from the base. Beyond that, he could see the highway that led to Larsborg.

Nothing. No traffic. Empty, for a mile.

During the few weeks he'd been in South Haakovia, Bolan had already had a couple of low-level problems with Markus. Nothing big, and certainly nothing blatant. Just little bureaucratic screwups, the blame for which couldn't be pinned on anyone in particular.

The question was, were the screwups intentional? Maybe. The Executioner had spent enough time in the military to know that the problems he encountered with Markus smelled of what was known as "vicious compliance."

Vicious compliance. You did what you were told. You followed your orders exactly as they were given to you, to the letter so that nobody could say you hadn't done your job.

But you made sure that somewhere along the line, a monkey wrench or two got thrown into the assignment.

An A-18CF Hornet land-based attack fighter hit the runway and taxied toward the refueling area. Bolan watched the forty-foot wings, still thinking of Markus. So far, he hadn't figured out the general's intentions. On the surface at least, Markus didn't strike him as a traitor. The general had been totally loyal to Edvaard Varkaus. But Varkaus was dead, and there seemed to be a certain distance between the man and Janyte Varkaus.

It might be as uncomplicated as Markus simply not liking to take orders from a woman. Or it could be more complex. Regardless, it was another loose end that needed to be tied off.

One thing had been perfectly clear since he arrived in Larsborg. Markus didn't like Colonel Rance Pollock.

Why?

The answer was simple. The general had been in charge of South Haakovia's military forces before the Executioner's arrival. Varkaus's request for American aid had brought Bolan in with equal, if not superior, power to the general.

General Gustaf Markus was jealous.

Bolan's eyes flickered back to the highway as a transport truck turned onto the gravel road. Grimaldi came around the side of the Tomcat. "Think that's it?" he asked.

Bolan shrugged.

The truck turned onto the base and headed toward the mess area. The driver got out of the vehicle carrying a clipboard and disappeared inside. He returned a few minutes later with three men in white aprons and began unloading cardboard boxes.

Bolan lifted the field phone and dialed the mess hall. "This is Pollock," he said into the instrument. "That driver bring anything for me?"

"Just a moment, sir."

The Executioner heard muffled voices on the other end. Then the voice said, "No, sir, Colonel. Just kitchen supplies."

Bolan hung up and looked at the sun on the horizon. If he didn't leave immediately, he'd have to postpone his photo recon of North Haakovia until tomorrow. But that was impossible. With Varkaus's assassination, the time bomb had been set. Each second, it ticked closer to the North Haakovian invasion no one doubted was coming. And when the moment of truth arrived, the intel he gained on this mission would be vital to counterstrikes.

The warrior turned to Grimaldi. "Let's go, Jack. I'll have to make do."

The ace flyboy reached out and grabbed his arm. "I try never to interfere, Striker," he said. "But you know what that means?"

Bolan stared him in the eye. He tapped the camera case hanging from his black nylon web belt. "Just that I'll have to get closer to shoot."

He vaulted into the seat behind Grimaldi and closed the canopy. Shrugging into his parachute, he pulled the goggles over his eyes and they taxied toward the runway.

And it meant one other thing, he thought grimly as the Tomcat lifted off.

As soon as he returned, it would be time to get a few things straightened out with General Gustaf Markus.

MULTIHUED FLOWERS sparkled like colored diamonds in the gardens outside the United Nations complex. They were matched by the colors of more than one hundred and fifty countries whose flags circled the entrance to the grounds.

One flag, drab by comparison and showing the map of the world from the North Pole, stood out among its brighter neighbors. It was as if this flag of simple blue and white bore no need to be noticed, so through its very lack of pretention it became the one on which the visitor's eyes fell first.

It was the flag of the United Nations, and it symbolized the international family that the world was capable of creating, not the disunity and chaos that the nations *had* created.

Carl Lyons opened the door of the limousine. His nostrils flared as the wind whipped over the East River, bringing with it a damp, musky odor. While the five South Haakovian diplomats exited the vehicle, the Able Team leader's eyes skirted the area, traveling from the low rectangular conference building to the glass and marble Secretariat. Squinting behind the lenses of his dark glasses, he mentally divided the thirty-nine stories for inspection.

Window upon window, floor after floor, met his gaze, and the cop that remained in Carl Lyons couldn't help wondering if snipers lurked behind every pane of glass as well as on the roofs. He closed the door and nodded to the four Secret Service men assigned to him. They fanned out, enveloping the Haakovians like linemen protecting a quarterback.

Lyons took the point, his eyes scanning the gardens as they neared the door to the General Assembly. The no-win assignment Able Team had been handed had become worse than even he had expected. It wouldn't have, had he, Schwarz and Blancanales been dealing with normal human beings. If these had been average, reasonable men in the center of the protection column, it would have been a simple matter of setting up security at the hotel and providing safe escort to and from the UN where security was always tight. He, Pol and Gadgets could have handled it themselves, with a few G-men in the wings as backup.

The big ex-cop opened the door to the General Assembly building with his left hand, his other sneaking unobtrusively inside his jacket and closing around the rubber grips of the Colt Python holstered under his arm. He stepped back as two of the Secret Service men filed past, followed by the diplomats. The other pair of G-men brought up the rear.

But they weren't protecting average men. Able Team was baby-sitting diplomats, which spelled "politicians," which as far as Lyons could see also spelled "spoiled children."

Their country at the northern tip of the Baltic Sea might be no bigger than Rhode Island, but the men from Larsborg had egos the size of Alaska.

Lyons hurried back to the point position. He started down the hall, his eyes flying over art exhibits from around the world. Under other circumstances, he might have enjoyed studying the paintings, busts and statues for their artistry, but right now his interest was far more pragmatic.

Each bust and statue large enough to hide a man might do just that. Each painting on the wall could conceal a timed or electronically detonated explosive, and every innocent-looking man and woman they passed on their way to the General Assembly hall could be a killer in disguise.

One might even be Dag Vaino.

Lyons continued to lead the way, wondering exactly what it was that caused politicians to get their priorities so out of whack. Not just the South Haakovians, but ninety percent of the statesmen he'd worked with over the years. The men from Larsborg had been a royal pain in the butt from the word go. They refused to wear the ballistic nylon vests Able Team had brought for them. They refused to change hotels and register under assumed identities.

And the suggestion that they remain in a guarded room and broadcast their speeches over closed circuit TV? The Able Team leader might as well have slapped them all in the face. "We cannot serve our country from a prison!" had become their buzz phrase.

Well, Lyons failed to see how the South Haakovians planned to serve their country dead. And he suspected they weren't so afraid of missing out on the opportunity to serve their country as they were on the publicity they were getting.

Free camera time didn't hurt the old career.

The ex-cop picked up the pace as they neared the door to the General Assembly. Behind him, he heard Lasse Kristofferson, a fat Haakovian wearing a brown suit, say, "What is the hurry? Are you trying to kill us for Stensvik?"

Lyons ignored him. When they reached the door, he flashed the Justice Department credentials he'd been issued and hurried inside, reconning the room before motioning the party to follow. As the five diplomats moved down the aisles to their seats, he saw Schwarz and Blancanales seated near the front with the Secret Service team assigned to North Haakovia.

The ex-cop shook his head in disgust. Years of police work had taught him that nothing ever went as planned, and this job had been no exception. The President's original plan had been for Able Team to protect the South Haakovians, but as soon as Stensvik's men had gotten word that the U.S. was providing extra security for the South, they'd demanded it as well. Their story was that the South Haakovians were after *them*.

So the presidential order had been amended, and Lyons had been forced to split his men into two factions.

Lyons took a final glance around the General Assembly room, then dropped into his seat as the secretary-general called the meeting to order.

Yes, he thought, his gun hand resting under his jacket. The security around both countries had been doubled.

But by dividing Able Team, they'd cut the South Haakovian's chances of survival by half.

THE COLD SCANDINAVIAN AIR was even colder at five thousand feet, and as he fell through the night, Yakov Katzenelenbogen thanked God it was still autumn in Finland. He wasn't getting any younger, and every morning old injuries—bullet holes, knife wounds, and especially the stub of arm at the top of his prosthetic limb—reminded him of the violent life he'd led.

Katz pulled the ripcord and his chute blossomed, jerking him up momentarily before allowing him to float downward again. He glanced to his right in the blackened sky. Vague outlines jerked in the air as the other members of Phoenix Force pulled their cords. Straining to look below, he saw the cargo chutes, still a hundred yards above the water. They had fallen on static lines and would reach the frigid sea a few minutes before the men.

The Phoenix Force leader adjusted the neck of his dry suit, shoved the regulator leading to the air tank into his mouth and tightened the mask over his eyes and nose. Everything ready now except the buoyancy unit, the Israeli tapped the button on his console and heard air rush into the vest.

Thirty seconds later, his fins hit the water.

The momentum of the fall drove Katz down through the water, then the air in his vest popped him back to the surface. He pulled the regulator from his mouth as he settled to a steady float. He watched the rest of the team disappear beneath the dark waves then pop back up like bobbins attached to a fishing line.

Katz disconnected his lines, folded his parachute and attached several lead sinkers to the wet nylon. He watched the chute sink out of sight through the dark water, then made his way to the nearest floating box. The cargo chute had fallen over the foam-lined plastic crate, and rather than waste time disentangling it, the Phoenix Force leader drew the Cold Steel Trail-master bowie knife from the sheath on his calf and sliced through to the lid. Katz opened the crate and removed the rubber dinghy. He inflated it with compressed air from the tank on his back, fixed the motor and other equipment into place, then stabbed holes through the bottom of the crate and sent it to join his chute at the bottom of the Gulf of Finland.

In his peripheral vision he watched Encizo, James, McCarter and Manning doing the same with their own rubber rafts.

The Israeli flipped on his wraparound walkie-talkie and spoke into the mike in front of his face. "Phoenix One... Two through Five. Everyone copy?"

The other four men responded.

"Then let's move out," Katz said, crawling over the side of the rubber raft. He touched the electric start button on the encased inboard motor and heard the near-silent hum as it kicked to life. Strapping himself into the seat, he took a reading from the compass on his scuba console. Then, grabbing the tiller, he adjusted the direction and started forward.

The other four rubber boats fell in behind.

Katz led the pack through the chilly water, the wind whipping around his neck to send chills beneath the dry suit. He thought briefly of the first two parts of the mission that lay ahead. Initially Phoenix Force's job was to infiltrate Finland, proving to the government in Helsinki that if they could do it, Stensvik could, too.

Stony Man was hopeful that this would promote more cooperation between the Finns and the Americans.

But as he moved slowly across the frigid waves of the Gulf of Finland, Katzenelenbogen knew that the first lap of the race would be the easy part. Finding and killing Dag Vaino came next, and Vaino had proved to be as slippery as an eel wearing sunscreen.

The Phoenix Force leader breathed easily as the convoy of dinghies hummed on. They had a lead. Not a great one, but at least someplace to start. Kurtzman had tapped into CIA intel just before they'd left Stony Man Farm. The spooks suspected that Dag Vaino had targeted either Risto Kalle, an outspoken anti-Haakovian member of Finnish parliament, or Leon Badzinski, the Ukrainian ambassador to Finland, for assassination.

Step two would be to hurry to Helsinki and make sure neither of those assassinations took place.

The radar sensor mounted to the front of the dinghy suddenly flashed red. Katz relaxed his hand on the throttle and the raft slowed. A moment later, a rock formation appeared above the sea. "Got one ahead," he whispered into the walkie-talkie. "Bear left, ten degrees."

Circling the protruding rocks, Katz readjusted his course and opened up the motor again. Fifteen minutes later, the lights of Porkkala, a Finnish coastal village two miles to their west, appeared vaguely through the fog.

Katz heard the distant roar of a power craft. He looked across the water to his right to see another light bearing down hard on them from the east.

"Craft at three o'clock," the Israeli whispered into his mike.

Calvin James's voice came back. "Finnish coast guard?"

"That or navy. Too far away to tell." Katz paused. "But even if it's nothing more than a fishing boat, we don't need them reporting us . . . yet."

"Affirmative."

Katz released the throttle and shoved the motor out of gear. The craft slowed, drifting through the water. He tapped a button on his console, and air began to bleed from the hull. "Submerge," he ordered. "Follow your compass readings until you hear from me again." He shoved the regulator back into his mouth, pulled the mask down over his eyes and nose, and a moment later, the rubber dinghy dropped beneath the surface.

Katz grasped the console and stared at the luminous dial of his depth regulator. When it read thirty feet, he pumped enough air back into the dinghy to reach neutral buoyancy, shoved the motor back in gear and the open-top rubber submarine inched forward.

The sea floor appeared five minutes later, forcing Katz to rise to twenty feet. His eyebrows lowered beneath the mask. That was cutting it close if the oncoming boat happened to pass directly overhead. Depending on what kind of craft it was, and its displacement, he could find himself riding the rest of the way to Finland as the Headless Boatman.

Suddenly the dinghy began to vibrate. Cutting the throttle, the Israeli bled more air from the hull and dropped to the bottom.

Katz doubled forward as the dinghy continued to shake, the whirling blades above threatening to capsize the fragile craft and scatter the equipment across the ocean floor. He spread his arms, shifting his weight back and forth as the blades passed three feet above his head, slashing through the water like the teeth of angry sharks.

In seconds the boat passed on.

Katz threw the dinghy back in gear and started forward. He gave it five more minutes before unstrapping the collapsible periscope and extending the metal tubing to the surface. Twisting the lens through a quick 360-degree arc, he saw no signs of the craft. He pressed the small button mounted to the side of his walkie-talkie and felt the vibration as the sonar signal passed from his radio to the rest of Phoenix Force.

The five dinghies rose as one to the surface.

The shore was visible now through the fog, and the Israeli opened the throttle, gliding over the waves until he was within ten feet of the rocky beach. He tore the mask from his face.

Manning, McCarter, Encizo and James pulled their rafts to a halt behind him. Quickly the Stony Man warriors unloaded their equipment, turned the dinghies around, tied down the tillers and threw them into gear. The small rubber crafts started slowly back out to sea.

When the rafts had floated two hundred yards in deep water, Katz pulled a remote control from his backpack. He tapped a series of buttons, and five tiny explosions sounded across the waves. Although he couldn't see them in the darkness, he knew the dinghies were already sinking beneath the surface and away from detection.

Manning stepped up next to him, staring out over the blackened sea. "Kind of a shame, isn't it?" he said to no one in particular.

"What's that?" McCarter asked.

"Having to get rid of the rafts like that. They were really kind of fun."

Katz thought of the blades that had almost decapitated him and suppressed a laugh. "Let's go," he said, turning, and the men of Phoenix Force followed him up the beach.

A LITTLE OVER two hundred miles northeast of the Finnish shore where Katz and his men had landed, a figure fell through the sky above North Haakovia. Darker than the night itself in combat blacksuit and nylon assault boots, Mack Bolan hit the ground running, a mile south of Sturegorsk.

Scanning the area as he hauled in his chute, the warrior saw the edge of a thick pine forest to the west, the waters of Lake Ladoga to his east. He wondered briefly if Phoenix Force had encountered any problems entering Finland, then pushed the worries from his mind.

Katz and his men were big boys, and they were as good as they came. He had handpicked the team himself years earlier when the Stony Man operation had first come into existence, and they had never let him down. They would give it their all, and if necessary, go down fighting.

Bolan wrapped the cords around the chute and held it against his chest as he sprinted into the trees. Then, dropping the bundle of black nylon on the ground, he pulled an entrenching tool from his backpack and dug swiftly through the soft damp soil. As soon as the hole was deep enough, he dropped the chute inside and covered it.

The warrior stood, opened his backpack and pulled out a wool overcoat and Russian hare *shrapki* from inside. He shrugged into the coat, pulled the side flaps of the hat down over his ears and stepped from cover.

The lights of the North Haakovian capital beckoned in the distance. Breaking into a jog, the Executioner paralleled the road, ready to dive back into the concealment of the pines should headlights appear.

As he ran, Bolan took mental inventory of the equipment hidden under his coat. His standard weapons, the Desert Eagle .44 Magnum and Beretta 93-R, rode in their usual positions. The big Magnum was pulled tight against his hip on the nylon gun belt, and the 15-shot, select-fire 9 mm pistol was holstered under his arm. In addition to the handguns, Bolan carried six fragmentation grenades clipped within easy reach on his combat harness. A Cold Steel Magnum Tanto hung beneath the Beretta on the left side of his belt. The nearly nine-inch blade was resilient enough to be driven through a car door, yet sharp enough to sever the head from a man's body with one swift slash.

On the other side of his belt, behind the Desert Eagle, the Executioner carried a ToolClip, complete with wire cutter, pliers, saw blade, light-duty pry bar and other implements. The pockets of his blacksuit, as well as the flopping backpack, held a variety of other equipment that the warrior might need. A camera, and several rolls of lightning-fast night film on which he'd record his findings, had been transferred to a coat pocket.

He had everything he'd need.

Except the long-range lens.

A flash of light appeared on the road ahead, and the Executioner dived under the low boughs of a towering pine tree, drawing the sound-suppressed Beretta. He waited, staring through the branches, as more headlights rounded a curve ahead and fell in behind the lead vehicle. As the convoy drew near, he made out the distinctive lines of a Russian-made troop carrier in the shadows. As the trucks drew abreast, the freshly painted sickle-and-pine-tree insignia of Stensvik's Communist regime became clear on the vehicles' doors.

The convoy passed.

The Executioner stood and walked to the road. The city lay less than a half mile ahead now. The potential cover of the forest ended several hundred yards before that.

It was time to change tactics.

Pulling a camouflage bandanna from his pack, Bolan wiped the black cosmetics from his face and hands. He started down the road, walking briskly in the night chill.

He had taken less than a hundred steps when he saw more headlights flash from behind. The warrior moved to the side of the road, continuing to face ahead. The vehicle pulled to his side and stopped.

The old man behind the wheel called out to him in Haakovian.

The Haakovian language was a mixture of Swedish and Finnish, and dotted liberally with Russian slang terms picked up during the years of occupation. Bolan recognized it immediately.

The problem was, he neither understood nor spoke it.

The Executioner walked to the car, an aging Russian ZIL.

The old man behind the wheel rolled down the window.

Bolan pointed to his mouth and shook his head. *"Parlez-vous français?"* The last thing he needed at this point was to be tagged as an American.

This time, it was the old man who shook his head. "I speak a little English. Do you?"

"A little," the warrior replied in a French accent.

"Do you need a ride?"

"Oui."

The Executioner climbed into the car and the old man took off toward Sturegorsk, bragging about his position as a repairman with the North Haakovian version of AT&T. He was one of the few Haakovians who held a permanent "night pass" that enabled him to break with impunity the curfew Stensvik had imposed. As if a light bulb had suddenly gone on in his head, he turned to the Executioner. "And what are *you* doing out at night?"

Bolan thought fast. "I am, er, how you say... architect. Here to build. Looking over the area."

The old man was more concerned with himself, and the flimsy story seemed to satisfy him. He went back to bragging about his indispensability to the phone company.

The warrior listened politely, nodding and answering a question occasionally.

They hit the outskirts of Sturegorsk, then drove through several residential areas. The rule of the night seemed to be silence.

The streets of the capital were as vacant as the surface of the moon. Only a few lights shone through the closed curtains in the windows of houses.

The old man let Bolan out in front of the Hospiz hotel, a shabby two-story building near the center of town. As soon as he'd pulled away, the Executioner took a scrap of paper from his picket: 423 Mannerheim, the address read. Goran Englebretson.

The warrior made his way through the downtown area, passing the closed stores and encountering no other pedestrians. With the curfew in effect, North

Haakovia was hardly the party capital of the Baltics. All but the most daring stayed off the streets at night.

The curfew made him stick out like a sore thumb, and the Executioner cut down a side street at the first opportunity. The next person he encountered might be more interested than the old man that a French architect was on the streets. He quickened his step.

According to Stony Man intel that Kurtzman had picked up through the CIA, Goran Englebretson led a small pack of resistance fighters in North Haakovia. Brognola had used the spooks to notify Englebretson that an American agent would be infiltrating the country. Englebretson had agreed to lead the Executioner to strategic military sites. The freedom fighter had even volunteered to photograph the installations himself and smuggle the pictures to the South, but Bolan had refused.

He wanted to see the sites as well as photograph them. Photos without firsthand knowledge, the Executioner knew, could be misleading. So Englebretson had agreed to meet him at the house on Mannerheim with several of his men. The lights would be off, and Bolan was to go to the back door and knock six times.

The Executioner entered another tattered residential section. Two blocks later, he found Mannerheim. He turned the corner and stopped in his tracks.

Ahead, he saw the house. The numerals 423 were illuminated above the front door by the porch light. But the lights inside the house were all on as well, and parked outside along the curb, in the driveway and in the yard itself were half a dozen North Haakovian army jeeps.

TREPIDATION FLOODED Janyte Varkaus's soul as the limousine turned the corner and slowed in front of the Thorenson building. Her fingers traced the cold hard surface of the rectangular object inside her open purse.

When the time came, could she force herself to use it? Or would she shrink from what she knew to be her duty if South Haakovia was to keep from splintering into special-interest factions now that her husband was gone?

Janyte closed her eyes. Her pulse raced. Edvaard's body was hardly cold, and already the government threatened to dissolve. True, all of the separate factions might oppose the Communist North, but their disunity would nevertheless aid Stensvik's coming invasion.

The driver brought the vehicle to a stop, and South Haakovia's new president took a deep breath. She had a job ahead of her, the type of job at which her husband had not only excelled, but in which he seemed to take perverse pleasure.

But would she be able to pull it off? Deep in her heart, Janyte feared she might not.

She stayed in the back seat, letting Hans and Igor open both rear doors. The two burly bodyguards General Markus had assigned to her got out. Igor glanced up and down the street, then stuck his head back in and nodded.

Janyte threw the strap of her purse over her shoulder and slid across the seat to accept his outstretched hand. As he helped her onto the sidewalk, she saw eight more men with rifles hurrying toward her from the vehicles in front of and behind the limo. The team surrounded her as she walked up the sidewalk.

The men shot anxious glances ahead, above and to the sides as Janyte started up the steps. Suddenly she felt the urge to laugh. The last time she'd been in the presence of this much nervous testosterone had been in high school back in Estonia, when dozens of boys had vied for the privilege of escorting her to the senior dance.

Igor opened the front door to the Thorenson building, then ushered her inside. A guard wearing a beret of the South Haakovian Special Forces hurried to the elevator and pushed the call button. Janyte floated along in the midst of her protective shell as the doors rolled open.

The same man in the beret pressed the button for the fourth floor as the doors closed again. The elevator rose, and Janyte called to mind Quenby Knudsen's leering face.

Of all the factions threatening to split from her leadership, Knudsen's was the most vocal. As minister of the interior, he had entertained hopes of replacing Edvaard Varkaus himself. He had openly opposed the emergency session of parliament that had placed her in power, and released press statements about her that were not only distasteful, but false and bordered on treasonous.

Knudsen had also ignored her official request that he come to the castle to discuss their differences.

So Janyte Varkaus had gone to him.

The elevator doors opened, and the man in the beret led the pack toward the frosted glass door at the end of the hall. Twisting the knob, he stood back while several of the men entered, surveyed the surroundings, then turned back and nodded.

Janyte and Igor walked inside.

A short gray-haired woman sat behind the desk in the reception area. Her mouth dropped open in astonishment as the South Haakovian president stepped in. "Madam... President?" she gasped.

Janyte felt a new strength come over her. "How nice of you to notice," she said. "Inform Minister Knudsen that I am here to speak with him."

The woman fingered her hair self-consciously. "Do you have an... I mean... was he expect—"

Janyte looked her square in the eye. "I do *not* have an appointment. Nor do I need one," she said in a voice she hardly recognized as her own. "You would do well to remember that Quenby Knudsen works for me, not the other way around."

The woman's hand flew to the phone at her side. She mumbled into the receiver, then recradled it. "Minister Knudsen will see you in a moment."

Janyte started to speak, then stopped. If she wasn't careful, she'd take her anger out on this poor faultless woman who was just another victim of Knudsen's arrogance. She nodded and took a seat along the wall. Igor, Hans and the soldier in the beret stood next to the door while the rest of the bodyguards formed a standing circle around her.

Janyte's hand crept inside her purse again, reassuring herself that the cold hard object was still there. Another wave of anxiety swept over her.

Her mind flew from Larsborg to her home in Estonia. Long ago, when she'd been a little girl in Talinn, her father had taught her to concentrate on pleasant things when fear threatened to overcome her, to use this mild form of self-hypnosis not as an escape, but to regain her balance and put things back into perspective.

Yes, the South Haakovian president thought silently. Pleasant things. Well, it would be pleasant to simply give up this position and return to Estonia. Let the Haakovians work out their own problems and again become nothing more than a diplomat's daughter.

The possibility hit her like a lightning bolt. Why not? After all, she wasn't Haakovian by birth, only by marriage.

The answer was just as jarring. No. She couldn't leave. Her father had taught her more than just how to relax when frightened, and one of those things was to accept responsibility when it was rightfully hers. Whether she wanted it or not.

As the seconds turned to minutes, Janyte's thoughts drifted to her husband. She had met Edvaard Varkaus when he'd still been the Haakovian ambassador to Estonia. Barely eighteen, she had been enamored by the hard handsome looks of the man nearly twenty years her senior, and flattered that such an important, high-ranking official was so obviously taken by her. Against her father's wishes they had married, and when Edvaard rose to the presidency, she had been at his side. Now he lay in state at the funeral home. Sometime soon, he would be moved to the castle chapel and readied for the services the day after tomorrow. Janyte tried to conjure up some form of sadness over his death.

And was successful. But no more so than she would have been had Edvaard been a distant acquaintance.

Janyte sighed. That was exactly what he had become over the years—distant. The infatuation she had mistaken for love as a young girl had worn off quickly as she got to know her husband. He was a democrat, all right, and fought hard against Communist aggression. But in many ways he himself had been almost as bad as the Stalinists, using the same underhanded tricks to get his way.

Guilt now replaced the anxiety in Janyte Varkaus's heart. She was about to employ one of those underhanded tricks herself.

The South Haakovian president looked down at her watch and saw that ten minutes had gone by. Well, enough was enough. What had to be done had to be done.

It was time to show Quenby Knudsen who was in charge of South Haakovia.

"Igor," Janyte said, rising to her feet and pointing, "open the door."

Igor moved to the door and twisted the knob. He turned back. "It is locked, Madam President."

"Then kick it down."

A thin grin crossed the bodyguard's lips as he stepped back. His foot shot forward, catching the door just below the lock. It swung inward.

Janyte Varkaus strode into Quenby Knudsen's office and closed the door behind her.

The walls of the minister's office were covered with framed prints. Knickknacks rested on every available surface. A television and videotape player stood against one of the walls, bookshelves lined the others. Knudsen sat behind a large oak desk, a pair of half glasses pinched to his nose. He glanced up briefly, then returned to the papers in front of him. "I will be with you in a moment," he muttered.

Janyte walked briskly across the room, leaned down and swept his desktop clean with a forearm. Papers, pencils and pens rattled to the floor. "You will be with me now, Minister Knudsen!" she shouted.

Knudsen leaned calmly back in his chair and let a smile play at the corners of his mouth. "Yes, Madam President," he said. "What can I do for you?"

Janyte stood before his desk. "To begin with, you may start supporting your government...working with it instead of against it."

"I am not against my government. I am only against its ineffectual leadership."

"When the crisis is over," she said, "there will be a free election. At that time you may support any candidate you choose. Or, as we both know is your ambition, you may seek the office yourself. But during this period, you will support those who are fighting to keep this country free."

Knudsen laughed without reservation. "And what will you do if I do not, my dear lady?" he asked. "Replace me? That would only strengthen my political position."

"There are other ways to handle you, Quenby Knudsen."

The smile vanished from Knudsen's face. "Assassination?" he said mockingly. "My dear little lady, I would have taken a threat like that to heart had it come from your husband. But from you, I cannot."

Janyte closed her eyes. She had tried reasoning, and as she had feared, it hadn't worked. An old expression of Edvaard's crossed her mind.

It was time to play her hole card.

"You are correct," she said. "Assassination is not in my nature." She reached into her purse and pulled out the object she had fondled earlier. "But when I am finished, death might very well be preferable to a man like you."

Knudsen's eyebrows lowered in interest.

Turning, Janyte walked to the wall, turned on the television and slipped the videotape in her hand from its cover. She shoved it into the front loader and punched the button.

The screen lighted up, showing the front entrance to a bar. A man dressed in a conservative gray suit came walking down the street. The picture was shaky and off-center, obviously taken by a camera hidden in a briefcase and shooting through a cutout in the leather. But it had been suitably efficient for the job, and as the man neared, Quenby Knudsen's face came into focus.

The camera followed Knudsen into the bar, to a table in a dimly lighted corner. A moment later, a hard-looking woman with long blond hair, a tight turtleneck sweater and a skirt so short the tops of her garter belt showed, took a seat next to the minister of interior. "You would like to have a date?" she asked in a husky voice.

Janyte turned back to the man behind the desk.

The color had drained from Knudsen's face, and the flesh around his mouth quivered slightly.

Small talk followed on screen, then Knudsen reached into his pocket, produced a wallet and counted off several bills. The camera followed him and the blonde out of the bar, down the street and up the steps of a seedy hotel.

Janyte turned back to Knudsen, who looked as if he might crawl under his desk at any moment. "You are married, are you not, Minister Knudsen?" She forced a smile. "I have never met your wife. Is this her?" She turned back to the television.

The picture faded to black, then returned, steadier, implying that the camera being used now was fixed. The scene had switched to the interior of a shabby hotel room. Cracks and craters in the plaster were the wall's only decorations. A bare striped mattress, filthy and torn, lay on the wrought-iron bed.

The woman with the blond hair smiled at Knudsen and pulled the turtleneck over her head. She licked her lips provocatively as she unzipped the skirt and let it fall to the floor at her feet. She pulled her silk camisole over her head and tossed it beside her skirt—revealing a flat hairy chest.

The black panties came off next, revealing a long erect penis.

The camera focused on the South Haakovian minister of the interior, who was seated on the bed. Knudsen's face was a mask of lust and anticipation.

Janyte Varkaus turned back to the desk. "I guess it is *not* your wife," she said. "I think I will leave you to watch the rest by yourself. It does nothing for me." She walked to the door and twisted the knob. "Do not bother returning the tape, Minister Knudsen. You may keep *that* copy."

The bodyguards stood waiting in the reception area. They reformed their cocoon and escorted the South Haakovian president down the elevator to the limousine. Janyte leaned back against the seat as Hans and Igor climbed in on both sides.

She had done what she had to do to keep her country together. And inconsistent with her fears, she *had* been good at it.

But she had been right in her other prediction. She didn't like these things the way Edvaard had.

The limousine pulled away from the Thorenson building. Janyte closed her eyes. Her fear was gone. So was her anger. But now a deep, gnawing sorrow filled her heart.

And as the limo started back toward the castle, Janyte Varkaus leaned forward and wept.

3

The Cuban addressing the United Nations General Assembly droned on with distorted rhetoric Carl Lyons had hoped would die with the cold war. Every few sentences, a carefully rehearsed, theatrical passion caused the squatty Communist's voice to rise two octaves.

"South Haakovia is the latest in a long line of American puppet states," the Cuban shouted into the microphone before him. "For over two hundred years..."

"Yeah, yeah, yeah," Lyons muttered under his breath. "When you can't come up with any new lies, fall back on the old." The Able Team leader glanced along the line of South Haakovian delegates seated in front of him, waiting their turn. They looked every bit as bored with the worn-out propaganda as he was.

Lyons's eyes did a fast three-sixty of the assembly hall. Except for the uniformed guards in front of the doors and the plainsclothes Secret Service men seated to the sides, the exits were clear. Dividing the room into four sectors, he scanned quickly into each quadrant, then returned to give the rows of heads another thorough exam.

A Russian near the front of the room reached into his jacket, and Lyons stiffened. Then the man came out with a handkerchief and blew his nose.

Three rows up on the left, one of the Afghani delegates leaned forward. Lyons's finely tuned ears heard a briefcase open, then the rustle of papers. He moved on, covering the entire hall, then starting over yet again.

A flash of movement caught his eye across the room, and he focused on the North Haakovian section. Gunner Kalajoki, one of Stensvik's representatives seated in front of Schwarz, had risen and was shuffling toward the aisle.

The big ex-cop caught Schwarz's eye. Gadgets raised his hand to the side of his head and casually extended his index finger over his ear.

One. The man was going to the rest room. *Two* meant someone was sick. *Three* would have told the Able Team leader that Schwarz had no idea what was about to go down, and to get ready.

Lyons watched Secret Service Agents Toad Baker and Tom Karns rise and follow Kalajoki up the aisle. Suddenly, for no apparent reason, an uneasy feeling crept over the Able Team leader.

The meeting hadn't been in session for more than ten minutes. Hadn't Kalajoki's mother ever taught him to "go" before he left the house? Of course the North Haakovian delegate wasn't any spring chicken—he could have bladder or prostate problems. Still . . .

Lyons leaned toward Brad Hutchinson, the brawny agent seated next to him. ''I'm going to check the halls. Take over here.''

Hutchinson nodded his agreement.

He hurried up the aisle, nodding to the men at the door as he passed into the hall. He circled the assembly room, moving toward the exit through which Kalajoki and the Secret Service men had left. He passed a display of iron busts depicting past and present South African statesmen, rounded a corner, and saw Karns, Baker and Kalajoki enter a men's room farther down the hall.

The Able Team leader quickened his step, almost breaking into a jog. Something was wrong. He didn't know what, and he had no hard evidence to back up his suspicion. But raw instinct had saved Carl Lyons many times when he'd been a cop on the streets of L.A., and while he might not always understand it, he'd learned to trust that instinct over the years.

Reaching the men's room, he slowed. The Secret Service men might understand the intuition that told him something was about to happen, but Gunner Kalajoki never would. If Lyons crashed through the door with the Colt Python in his fist, the North Haakovian would interpret it either as an attack, overreaction, or just downright stupidity.

Lyons reached into the side flap pocket of his sport coat, wrapped his fingers around the hammer-shrouded Colt Agent .38, then opened the door.

Karns and Baker stood in front of the sinks along the wall, their right hands under their jackets.

"Where's Kalajoki?" Lyons asked.

Karns pointed to one of the stalls.

Lyons glanced down beneath the door and saw a pair of shoes and trouser legs.

"You check all the stalls before he went in?" Lyons asked.

Toad Baker stared back at him, expressionless. "We like to think we're halfway professional."

Lyons ignored his tone.

A few minutes later, the toilet flushed and Kalajoki emerged through the door zipping his pants. He moved to the sink, washed his hands and tore a paper towel from the dispenser.

Lyons opened the door and checked the hall. Without a word Kalajoki shot him a nasty glance and walked past.

The Able Team leader took the lead, Kalajoki behind him. Baker and Karns brought up the rear. The uneasy feeling in the ex-cop's chest increased with every step. He glanced over his shoulder at Kalajoki.

Something seemed different about the North Haakovian.

But what?

Lyons dropped back, taking up a position behind the man. As they neared the entrance, he suddenly recognized the change and wanted to kick himself for not seeing it earlier.

Kalajoki's suit coat had been buttoned before he entered the rest room. Now it was open. Had the North Haakovian simply forgotten to rebutton it?

No. It hung lower over his right shoulder.

The same way Lyons's own coat did when he carried the snub-nosed Colt in his pocket.

Lyons moved forward as Kalajoki reached the door, but both Baker and Karns crowded close to the North Haakovian, blocking him off. Kalajoki's head swiveled, and the look in his eyes told Lyons even more than the hand that shot into the sagging pocket.

"Move!" Lyons screamed, grabbing Baker by the shoulders and shoving him to the side.

Karns turned toward him. "What—"

Lyons drove a shoulder into the Secret Service man's gut, cutting off his words and knocking him away. He charged through the door to the General Assembly hall in time to see Gunner Kalajoki sprinting down the aisle toward the South Haakovian section, a nickel-plated Colt Government Model .45 automatic in his hand.

THE EXECUTIONER DUCKED behind a parked car as another North Haakovian jeep rounded the corner behind him. The vehicle passed, and in the dim glow of the overhead streetlights he made out the silhouettes of more North Haakovian infantrymen armed with Russian AK-74 and Hungarian NGM assault rifles.

Bolan peered around the car as the jeep stopped in front of 423 Mannerheim and the soldiers hurried inside.

The warrior's face tightened as he assessed the situation. Okay, something had gone wrong. Somehow Stensvik had gotten wind of the safehouse where he was to meet Goran Englebretson and the rest of the freedom fighters. How? He didn't know, and at this point he didn't care. It bore looking into eventually, but for now, there were more immediate problems.

Like how to get Englebretson and his men out of the house alive.

The Executioner reached into his pack, pulled out a small pair of infrared binoculars and scanned the front lawn and side of the house. Only the jeep's drivers stood outside as guards, and all four men seemed complacent about their duties. They had crowded into one jeep and sat smoking and talking in hushed voices.

Through the darkness, Bolan saw a glimmer of orange. Then the face of a man wearing corporal's stripes appeared inside the flame. The man lighted his cigarette, said something to the others, and they laughed.

Bolan turned to the house. The lights were on, but shades covered the windows. If he could get close enough, he might be able to peer around the edges, but from this distance he could see nothing.

The Executioner dropped the binoculars back into his pack. Okay. Two possibilities—direct assault or covert infiltration. A direct assault would demand he take out the men in the jeep, then create some type of diversion to distract the enemy inside the house.

If he decided to follow the covert path, it would mean entering the house disguised as an N.H. regular. He would still have to neutralize the drivers in the front yard, and hope one of their uniforms fit.

Advantages and disadvantages both way.

The Executioner made the decision in a heartbeat. Take care of step one. Then decide on the best course of action.

Bolan drew the sound-suppressed Beretta 93-R from under his arm with his right hand. Flipping the selector to 3-round burst, he leaned forward on his belly and crawled from behind the car. The hushed voices in the jeep grew louder as he used his elbows to drag himself across the lawns of the two houses separating him from number 423.

A hundred feet from the jeep, he heard the four men break out in laughter again. Good. They felt secure. They were paying no attention.

The Executioner eased to his feet.

Four heads turned as one as Bolan sprinted forward, the drivers digging for their hardware. The first tap of the warrior's trigger finger sent a burst of 9 mm parabellums through the surprised face behind the wheel. Without breaking stride, the Executioner turned the weapon toward the corporal and squeezed again, the rounds drilling through the man's sternum.

Bolan was less than ten feet from the jeep when the man riding shotgun raised his NGM. The warrior swung the 93-R his way, tapping another trio of rounds into his face. The assault rifle fell to the pavement with a metallic clank, and Bolan turned to the final man in the back seat.

The last soldier wore the look of death even before the Executioner pulled the trigger. His eyes had already receded into the sockets, his jaw fallen slack and loose. The NGM in his hands rose slowly, as if the arms holding it had already begun to rot.

Bolan helped him meet his destiny with another burst from the Beretta. Three more 9 mm rounds sliced through the N.H. soldier's chest. But the man's index finger had found the assault rifle's trigger, and as he jerked spasmodically in his death throes, the muscles in his hand froze.

A steady stream of 5.56 mm rounds exploded noisily from the barrel.

The Executioner dived forward under the burst. He emptied the magazine into the shooter's chest with no effect. The NGM kept firing, finally running dry of its own accord.

Bolan rose and sprinted toward the house. There would be no silent infiltration now. A direct assault was the only possibility.

Dropping the near-empty magazine from the Beretta, the Executioner shoved a fresh load up the butt as he ran. A North Haakovian sergeant stuck his nose out the door as the warrior hit the slide release and simultaneously leaped onto the porch.

The Executioner's next 3-round burst drilled through the curious nose and drove the man back into the house. The warrior vaulted over the body as he hit the entryway. He saw two pairs of men dressed in civvies seated on the floor and tied back to back.

Half a dozen soldiers stood gaping around them.

The N.H. regulars came out of their shock, grabbing for their weapons as Bolan hit the floor on his knees. A tall blond lieutenant drew a Walam 48-M from his hip holster and snapped two 9 mm Shorts over the Executioner's head. Bolan raised the Beretta and got off a volley of hollowpoints that dropped the man in his tracks.

The Executioner reached behind his back and drew the Desert Eagle with his left hand as an N.H. private jerked the Danuvia 43-M from the sling across his back. A torrent of 9' × 25 mm Mauser rounds flew from the Hungarian-made subgun, dotting the wall next to the Executioner.

The Desert Eagle roared, the recoil driving Bolan's hand back as the big .44 drilled a Magnum round through the private's skull. The man flew back as if he'd been hit between the eyes with a baseball bat.

The warrior fell to his side as a rainstorm of rounds from two more 43-Ms sailed his way. Firing the Beretta and Desert Eagle simultaneously, he dropped a soldier wearing a floppy boonie hat, and a short, stocky man with a bushy mustache. He saw a grossly overweight soldier turn tail and dart through a side door into a hall. The Desert Eagle boomed again, sending two more massive .44s through the chest of an N.H. infantryman wrestling with a jammed pistol.

The last man standing in the room was in his early twenties. He dropped the subgun in his hands, threw them into the air and screamed. Bolan glanced toward the door where the fat soldier had disappeared, and as he did, he saw the young man's arms begin to fall.

The 7.65 mm pistol was halfway out of the guy's holster when the Executioner's Beretta took him out of the action.

Bolan jammed the Beretta into his belt. Transferring the Desert Eagle to his right hand, he moved cautiously toward the door to the hall. He had heard no outside doors open, no windows slide up, since the fat man left the room.

Which meant he hadn't gone far.

The Executioner kept the .44 close to his side as he dropped to one knee. He was about to risk a glance around the corner when he heard the soft breathing on the other side of the wall.

Bolan froze.

No, the enemy hadn't gone far. In fact he was less than six inches away, just around the corner, hidden only by the thin Sheetrock.

The warrior didn't hesitate. Twisting at the waist, he drove the Desert Eagle's heavy barrel through the wallboard. White dust drifted up through the air as his hand disappeared into the hall. The barrel hit something soft.

The Executioner pulled the trigger.

Deeply imbedded in the fat man's belly, the explosion sounded dull on the other side of the wall. Bolan rose to his feet and stepped through the door, the Desert Eagle leading the way. He looked down to see the fat soldier moaning, blood pouring from the crater in his gut.

The reason the man had darted from the room, then hidden so closely, became apparent as the Executioner's eyes fell on the open breach of the subgun at his feet. The man had run out of ammunition. But the handle of the twelve-inch fighting knife with which he'd planned to skewer the Executioner was still gripped in his fingers.

Bolan dropped the sights on the soldier's forehead as the fat man struggled toward a final attempt. Cursing in Haakovian, he raised the knife over his head and prepared to throw.

The Executioner's blast eliminated the man's face. The fighting knife fell from his fist.

The warrior stepped back into the living room, for the first time getting a chance to take a good look at the bound men. In general they looked like most of the natives of both North and South Haakovia, with either Scandinavian or Slavic features or a mixture of both. They wore rough cotton shirts and trousers, and one of the men, gray-headed and wearing round spectacles, had tall, moccasin-style "Lapp" boots on his feet. Blood ran down both his cheeks, and the Executioner looked down to see an N.H.-issue survival knife on the floor.

Dark red blood streaked the blade. The torture-interrogation had been just beginning when the Executioner had arrived.

Bolan knelt and picked up the knife. "You're Englebretson?" he asked as he sliced through the ropes that held the man's feet together.

The gray head nodded. "And you are Colonel Rance Pollock?" He held out his hands, and the Executioner drew the blade between them, severing the thong.

"That's right." He moved to the side, and cut the rope that bound Englebretson to the man seated behind him.

"Normally I would ask for some verification," Englebretson said, his eyes skirting over the bodies littering the room, "but I think you have already verified your identity."

Bolan moved to the other pair of men and began freeing them. He shrugged. "At least you know I'm a friendly."

"Yes."

Englebretson and the man behind him stood, rubbing their wrists to regain circulation. As Bolan cut through the restraints on the other two freedom fighters, they began collecting the weapons from around the room.

The Executioner stood with the other two. "We'd better get out of here. There may be more men coming any—"

Four more North Haakovian army jeeps suddenly roared down the street and skidded into the front yard to finish the warrior's thoughts.

THE SOUTH FINLAND COAST reminded Yakov Katze-nelenbogen of the shores of the Brac, the second of the three tiny dots in the Caribbean that made up the Cayman Islands. Rugged iron shore grew from the ground, spiraling into the foggy moonless night like accusing fingers.

The shore wouldn't be the only rough thing ahead for Phoenix Force, Katz mused as he led his men away from the water. Neither infiltrating Finland nor finding Dag Vaino was likely to prove easy. And killing the treacherous Finnish terrorist would be even harder. Two aspects of the situation would further complicate things, and by comparison make the iron shore now stabbing into his combat boots seem as smooth as glass.

First, Finland didn't want American help, and Phoenix Force would be considered the enemy if it was discovered. Second, Finland was not Phoenix Force's enemy, and that meant that the Stony Man warriors had no intentions of using lethal force on well-intentioned soldiers doing their jobs.

The sum of all this meant Katz and company would have one hand tied behind their backs throughout the mission. A hard grin edged across the former Mossad agent's face as he thought of Able Team at the UN. They'd be experiencing similar difficulties, he imagined, trying to deal with the Haakovian politicians.

A ship's horn sounded somewhere across the water. Katz glanced over his shoulder as he continued across the scraggly shore. Somewhere between him and the ship, Uzis slung over their shoulders and loaded down with the equipment they had taken off the rafts, the other members of the Stony Man team would be picking their way across the rough terrain. The men of Phoenix Force needed few orders—they'd fought together so long it sometimes seemed they were tapped into a central brain. Katz hadn't had to tell them to split up for the two-mile trek toward the highway; they had automatically spaced themselves far enough apart that if one was spotted, the others would still have plenty of time to conceal themselves.

Katz heard a soft footstep. He turned, and a tall silhouette appeared thirty yards behind him. Gary Manning, the rugged explosives expert who would probably be hunting big game in the Canadian wilderness if he wasn't engaged in this mission, moved quietly through the night. The outdoorsman carried a variety of detonation gear in his pack and vest, some of it lethal, the rest designed to delay, confuse or otherwise incapacitate without causing permanent trauma.

Behind Manning, Katz could see the vague outline of Rafael Encizo, nicknamed Pescado—fish in Spanish—by the other members of the team. What Manning did above water, Encizo handled below. An expert at underwater demolitions, the Cuban patriot was a survivor of both the Bay of Pigs and Castro's infamous El Principe Prison.

The Phoenix Force leader turned back toward the road. He couldn't see them in the darkness, but he knew the other two members of Phoenix Force were scattered behind Manning and Encizo.

Somewhere in the fog, ready and more than willing to engage in whatever came his way, was Calvin James. With a year of medical school under his belt before he became a cop, the black man often acted as Phoenix Force's unofficial medic. He was the team's best knife fighter, and had learned the ways of the blade as a tough youth on Chicago's South Side. Navy SEAL training had refined his technique.

The Israeli's thoughts turned to David McCarter, who was bringing up the rear of the column. The former British Special Air Service officer's apparently rigid demeanor was misleading to those who didn't know him well. Behind what appeared to be a stereotyped British stuffiness lay the ability to howl in glee or explode in anger, dependent upon the situation. McCarter could pilot anything with wings up to four engines, and his skill in the air was surpassed by very few men.

Ahead, through the foggy air of the south Finland night, Katz saw flickers of moving light. He stopped and tapped the button on the walkie-talkie. "Phoenix One," he said into the wraparound transmitter in front of his face. "Come on up." The former Mossad agent pulled a topographical map and Mini-Mag flashlight from the pocket of his BDU blouse. Cupping his hand around the flashlight's beam, he glanced down as the men of Phoenix Force gathered around. He tapped the map, then nodded toward the car headlights in the distance. "The road," he whispered. "The forest should start just the other side. Once we're inside the trees, it shouldn't be any big trick to follow the highway on in to Helsinki.'' He paused and squinted through the fog. "But there's movement out there tonight, and getting across without being spotted is going to be the problem.''

Manning tapped his backpack. "How about a small diversion?'' he said. "Something to stop traffic for a while?''

Katz nodded and pointed to the east. "Block it off a quarter of a mile up or so. Take McCarter with you.'' He turned to Encizo. "You think you can make things blow up if they aren't wet?''

The little Cuban grinned.

"You and Calvin head west, then. Same thing.''

"There'll be some cars trapped in between,'' James warned.

Katz shrugged. "We'll have to hope they're more interested in what's holding them up than five guys crawling under their wheels. I'll go on ahead and look for a good spot to cross. I'll move straight ahead and stop a hundred yards or so from the highway. Everybody meet there in thirty.''

The Israeli trudged on, crossing the craggy shore alone as the other members of Phoenix Force split off in opposite directions. When he was a hundred yards from the busy highway, he swung the Steyr machine pistol around to his back, dropped to his belly and pulled a pair of infrared binoculars from his pack.

The heavy traffic zoomed past. Katz strained, trying to look inside the vehicles. He caught fleeting glimpses of hats and scarves. Here and there, the head of a child.

Civilians, mostly. They weren't likely to pay much attention.

Then, just as he was about to return the binoculars to their case, three military vehicles passed. He couldn't make out the markings on the sides, but if they weren't army they'd belong to the Finnish equivalent of the border patrol.

Not that it mattered. Either spelled trouble for Phoenix Force.

Katz raised the binoculars slightly and gazed at the forest, ten yards on the other side of the road. He dropped the glasses, blinked, then stared at the terrain in front of him. The last hundred yards between the sea and highway turned to grassland, then a wide gravel shoulder paralleled the highway. Open country, except for a small row of conifers perhaps twenty yards this side of the highway. Not much in the way of cover.

But it would have to be enough. It was all they had. If they belly-crawled to the trees, set off the explosions, then made a break for it, Phoenix Force stood a fighting chance of not being spotted.

The Israeli rose to his feet, looped the neck strap over his head and let the binoculars fall to the end. A few minutes later, Manning and McCarter jogged across the rugged shore, their Uzis bouncing at the end of the slings.

Manning held a remote-control detonator in his hand. "All set," he said. "There'll be lots of noise and flying dirt. Ought to divert attention and be enough to slow things down for a minute or two without anybody getting hurt."

Katz nodded. "As soon as Rafael and Calvin get back, we'll move on up." He pointed toward the trees.

The men from Stony Man stood silently, waiting. Seconds turned to minutes, and as they did, a chill crept up the Israeli's spine. Encizo and James knew their business as well as any men on earth. The assignment he'd just given them wasn't complex, and they should have returned by now.

He raised his wrist and stared at the luminous face of his watch. Instead they were ten minutes late.

Something was wrong. He could feel it in his gut.

Katz tapped the button at his side and spoke into the headset. "Phoenix One . . . Two and Five. Come in, Two and Five."

He got no response.

The Israeli jerked the walkie-talkie from his belt and tapped another button on the side. A red light glowed dull in the darkness. "They've turned their radios off," he said.

McCarter's eyebrows lowered in concern. "That means they've got company."

Katz stared off in the direction Encizo and James had gone. The thick fog stared back. "Let's go," he said, breaking into double time. Manning and McCarter fell in behind him.

The Phoenix leader picked up speed, angling due west, estimating a quarter mile before turning toward the road. The car lights on the road could still be seen through the thick haze, but unlighted vehicles wouldn't be visible. If one of the passing military vehicles had chanced upon James and Encizo...

Ahead, Katz's ears picked up the sound as boots crunched on gravel. He slowed, his hand automatically gravitating to his belt, toward a nondescript, square leather pouch.

Before he could unsnap it, four shadowy forms stepped out of the mist.

A deep voice shouted what sounded like an order in Finnish.

Katz, Manning and McCarter froze in their tracks. None understood Finnish, but the bolts of four Sako-Valmet M-76 assault rifles sliding home in the stillness of night needed no translation.

A man wearing the uniform of a Finnish lieutenant stepped forward. He said something else, then frowned when the three men didn't respond. Switching to what Katz thought sounded like Haakovian, and still getting no response, he finally motioned for them to drop their weapons.

Katz's Steyr and the two Uzis fell to the ground.

The lieutenant gathered the weapons while the other three men circled behind Phoenix Force and jabbed the Valmets into their backs. They marched toward the road.

A few minutes later, the lights of the passing cars shone brightly through the fog. A dark form appeared. Katz squinted and the outlines of the three military jeeps came into focus.

Then, as they neared the road, more forms became distinct through the fog. Yakov Katzenelenbogen saw half a dozen Finnish soldiers with the crest of the coast guard emblazoned on their sleeves.

They stood aiming M-76s and Suomi-31 9 mm submachine guns at Rafael Encizo.

Katz's eyes scanned the roadside as the rifle in his back prodded him forward. Where was James? Had he hidden somewhere undetected? Perhaps he was even now circling and preparing to—

The answer to Katz's question came suddenly as he stepped over a large outcropping of iron shore. A dark, crumpled form appeared at the bottom of his vision, and he had to jump to the side to avoid stepping on it.

The Israeli ground to a halt. No, Calvin James wouldn't be coming to their rescue. Not tonight, anyway.

He lay in a heap on the ground, blood oozing from the deep laceration in his scalp.

A Finnish captain stepped from the circle of men around Encizo. His narrow black eyes were divided by a long thin nose that protruded from his gaunt face. Like the lieutenant, he spoke first in Finnish, then Haakovian, finally switching to English when Katz and the others shrugged. "You are Americans," he said. It was a statement rather than a question.

Katz exaggerated his Israeli accent when he answered. "We are *friends*."

The captain snorted. "We shall see." He looked toward the men around Encizo and said, "Gustoff, go and see if the black man is still breathing. The rest of you, handcuff them all and put them in the jeeps."

Katz stood silently as one of the men produced a set of handcuffs, spun Encizo and cuffed his wrists. Four others moved forward.

The former Mossad officer watched the cars passing on the highway slow to watch the show. He let his right hand drift slowly toward his belt and glanced at McCarter and Manning.

Both men nodded, knowing what their leader was thinking.

Katz's hand continued toward the belt pouch as the soldiers approached. The best chance of escape was always before the enemy had you fully secured, and in a few more moments the opportunity would disappear. The members of Phoenix Force might not end up in a Scandinavian prison for the rest of their lives, but by the time all the red tape had been sorted through, and the politicians on both sides of the Atlantic had blustered and swaggered their way to some agreement that allowed both Finland and the U.S. to save face, it would be too late for the mission.

Katz's thumb rose casually, flipping the snap. Out of the corner of his eye, he saw McCarter's and Manning's hands at the innocent-looking equipment pouches on their own belts. He waited, knowing his timing and aim would have to be perfect.

As the soldiers stepped into range, the three warriors drew simultaneously, like a gang of Old West bandits about to rob a bank. But the instruments that appeared in their hands were light-years away from the Colt Peacemakers that won the West.

Katz's index finger found the Taser's trigger, and the first of his two darts shot out to strike the nearest soldier in the chest. The Finn jerked spasmodically, as fifty thousand volts of electrical current shot through his body.

Gasps echoed to the man's side as McCarter and Manning launched their own Taser darts into two other soldiers. Katz turned his weapon on the fourth man. His second dart hit the soldier near the collarbone and knocked him to the ground.

McCarter and Manning had already ripped their wires from the chests of their victims and were sprinting toward the soldiers surrounding Encizo. As the captain raised his Valmet, Encizo's foot snaked out, catching him in the thigh. The kick ruined his aim, and the rifle round discharged harmlessly. McCarter launched his second dart into the captain's midsection, and the Finn dropped as if he'd been poleaxed.

Manning hit the ground rolling and came up with the Valmet. Coming to a halt in a kneeling position, he aimed the assault rifle at the remaining two soldiers and said, "Drop 'em."

Their weapons fell to the ground and they raised their hands.

Suddenly automatic fire whizzed over their heads. Katz and the rest of Phoenix Force ducked instinctively, then turned to see the man who had gone to check on James standing behind them. His subgun tracked left, then right, covering them all. "No," he said nervously, finally aiming the gun at Manning. "*You* will be the one to drop your weapon."

Slowly Manning began to lower the rifle. But as he did, the Finnish soldier suddenly jerked forward, closed his eyes and fell to the ground.

A shaky Calvin James appeared just behind the soldier, the barrel of his Beretta 92-S gripped in both hands. He blinked dizzily and held a hand to his forehead. "I miss anything important during my nap?"

Katz looked at Manning, who had already retrieved the Valmet and was covering the rest of the soldiers. "Okay," the Israeli said, addressing Phoenix Force as a whole. "Get them cuffed or tied and into the jeeps. Fashion some kind of gags. Pull the vehicles into the woods out of sight. By the time they've worked themselves free, we should be long gone." He watched a car on the highway slow, then speed up when the driver saw what had happened. "And hurry," he added. "Somebody may decide to be a good citizen and call in."

McCarter hurried to James, pulling a bandage and antibiotics from the medic's own kit and applying them to the head wound. "Superficial," he called out.

Katz nodded. The rest of the Stony Man warriors secured their prisoners.

As soon as the Finns were bound and out of sight in the trees, Katz walked up to the captain. "I want you to deliver a message for me."

The captain stared back silently above his gag.

"Tell your superiors that we are *not* the enemy. But if we can get through your defenses, so can Stensvik." He turned to the other members of the team. "Ready?"

Four heads nodded.

As Katz led his men into the forest, he heard Encizo behind him. "I never have understood how those Tasers work," the little Cuban whispered. "What are they, fifty thousand volts?"

"Yeah," Manning answered. "But it's not the volts that get you, it's the amps."

Somewhere to the rear, McCarter snorted. "Yes, it's not the heat, it's the humidity. But the sweat is just the same."

Katz smiled. The first leg of the mission had been accomplished. Now he had to concentrate on how to find Dag Vaino.

4

Gasps spread through the General Assembly as Lyons drew his Colt Python and sprinted down the aisle after Kalajoki. The Cuban speaker at the podium stopped talking, his bottom lip falling almost to his chest.

Secret Service agents, plainclothes and uniformed security officers rose in their seats, drawing Berettas and SIG-Sauers from under their jackets and aiming toward the running North Haakovian.

But the lawmen didn't fire.

The General Assembly was packed. Their shots stood a good chance of missing Kalajoki and killing one of the other three hundred international delegates.

Lyons dropped the Python's front ramp sight on Kalajoki's back as he ran. He started to squeeze the trigger, then let his finger fall back, the cylinder rolling to a halt. He had a clear shot, with nothing but the empty aisle ahead and at least three feet to both of Kalajoki's sides. But the Python was loaded with .357 Magnum, 125-grain jacketed hollowpoints. They would leave the Colt's four-inch barrel at approximately 1450 feet per second, and they wouldn't slow down much in the fifty or so feet it took to reach their target.

Which meant that if the Able Team leader's bullets struck soft tissue, they'd pass right through the North Haakovian. And if they hit bone, they could easily deflect and end up God knew where.

Without breaking stride, Lyons shoved the Python into his waistband. He had pulled within thirty feet of the overweight statesman when Kalajoki raised the nickel-plated Colt Government Model. The delegate aimed into the South Haakovian seats, snapping off a shot as he ran, the explosion from the gleaming .45 in his fist echoing off the walls of the General Assembly room.

The round sailed over Lasse Kristofferson's right shoulder and lodged in the back of a seat three rows down. Most of the diplomats around the assembly hall dived for cover beneath the seats. Others, including two of the South Haakovians, froze in fear.

Lyons kept running, gaining one step on Kalajoki with every two. He watched the inexperienced gunman fumble with the .45's recoil, then bring the weapon back down into play. From the corner of his eye the big ex-cop noted both Schwarz and Blancanales scurrying between the seats toward the action.

Lyons was still fifteen feet behind the diplomat-turned-assassin when Kalajoki squeezed the trigger again. He saw Schwarz leave his feet, dive over two rows of seats and plow headfirst into Sytre Tamm, a tall slender South Haakovian with a receding hair-line.

Tamm crumbled between the seats, Schwarz on top. Kalajoki's bullet sailed high over their heads and into the wall.

The assassin drew even with the rearmost row of the South Haakovian section and ground to a halt. He took his time, aiming low between the seats.

Lyons couldn't see the target, but in his mind's eye he envisioned some huddled South Haakovian with his arms clasped protectively over his head. The Able Team leader saw the tendons in the back of Kalajo-ki's hands tighten as the man prepared to squeeze the trigger again.

The Stony Man warrior launched himself forward, sailing through the air and down the aisle, his arms outstretched. As his shoulder struck Kalajoki in the ribs, he heard the explosion as the .45 went off again.

The North Haakovian's ribs cracked louder than the pistol as Lyons propelled him down the aisle. A sick-ening shriek of pain escaped the statesman's lips. The two men rolled to a halt in front of the proscenium at the front of the room.

The .45 clattered across the floor, and Lyons saw Brad Hutchinson sweep it up in a burly paw. He turned back to Kalajoki and shoved the man's face into the floor, then rolled him over onto his back and climbed on top. As the ex-cop's fist drew back over his shoulder, two thoughts crossed his mind.

He wondered first if the last shot had hit any of the South's representatives, or any of the other men in the room. And he remembered his orders not to harm *any* of the Haakovians under any circumstances.

Lyons's fist froze in midair. He stared down into Kalajoki's frightened eyes, the anger rushing through his veins as if propelled by fire hoses. On the stage overhead, he heard someone rap a gavel, and then the pandemonium behind him began to quiet. He looked up to see Blancanales at the podium, pounding the wooden hammer like Thor summoning thunder. Pol's voice reverberated over the sound system as if in a dream.

"Return to your seats! Everyone! Return to your seats and sit down!"

The Able Team leader lowered his fist. Slowly, carefully, he frisked Kalajoki for other weapons. Finding none, he grabbed the would-be assassin by the knot in his necktie and jerked him to his feet.

Baker and Karns joined Lyons and Hutchinson at the front of the room, each taking one of the North Haakovian's arms.

Lyons saw the indecision on both men's faces. They'd gotten the same orders Able Team had: treat the Haakovians, both North and South, with kid gloves.

Baker started to speak, then stopped.

"Get him out of here," Lyons ordered, shoving Kalajoki into Baker's arms. "Take him someplace in the building. A vacant room. And keep him under guard."

"Our orders were—"

"Do it!" Lyons yelled. He turned back to Kalajoki.

The color had reappeared in the North Haakovian's face as he became aware that he wouldn't be killed. The skin of his forehead was taut from the pain in his ribs, but the man's insolence had returned. "I enjoy diplomatic immunity," he shouted. "You cannot—"

Lyons reached down and dug his fingers into Kalajoki's flabby throat. Circling them around the man's windpipe, he pressed his nose into the North Haakovian's and growled, "You're lucky you're still breathing. Enjoy *that.*"

Kalajoki's eyes widened. He sputtered for words.

Lyons released the man and looked back at Karns. "Get him out of my sight before I *do* kill him," he said and turned up the aisle. Blancanales joined him. Lyons heard the secretary-general at the podium. "We will take a one-hour recess," the man said.

Schwarz fell in beside his team members halfway to the door. "Talk about your no-win situations, Ironman," the electronics man said in disgust.

"All these guys want protection, but they don't want to alter their life-styles one bit to get it," Blancanales added. "How are we supposed to keep them safe and not hurt anyone? Magic?"

Lyons didn't answer. He stopped at the door and turned back to his men. "Gadgets, go back to the North. Pol, take over for me with the South while I'm gone."

"Where are you going?"

"To make a telephone call. See if I can get some more help. If we've all got to fight this thing with one arm tied behind our backs, the least we can do is get some more one-armed men."

Shoving past the guards at the door, the Able Team leader stalked down the hall, the heat in his chest rising to the boiling point. Gadgets and the Politician were right. It was a no-win situation. Somebody was going to get killed before it was all over, and if the good guys weren't allowed to kill the bad guys, it meant the bad guys would kill them.

Lyons hurried past the row of South African busts, turned the corner and reached the telephone booth outside the men's room. He took a seat on the stool and swung the door closed behind him. Through the glass he saw three dark-skinned men stroll down the hall toward the General Assembly. Squinting, he recognized their Peruvian name tags.

The ex-cop dropped a quarter into the slot as the party passed the booth. His stiff, angry fingers practically drilled holes through the numbers for Stony Man Farm. As he waited for the line to connect, he continued to watch the Peruvians.

Barbara Price answered on the second ring. "Hello?"

Lyons hesitated, taking a deep breath to try to calm his frustration.

"Hello?" Price repeated.

Still eyeing the men in the hall, Lyons said, "Barbara, I need more men, and I need them now. One of the North's own diplomats just declared hunting sea-son on the South, and for all we know the South may be planning something in retaliation.''

Two men wearing olive green work shirts appeared from a side hall wheeling a cardboard box strapped to a dolly. Lyons's gaze narrowed as they paused to readjust their load next to the men from Peru.

A tall muscular workman walked over to the dark-skinned men, an unlighted cigarette dangling from his lips. One of the Peruvians, wearing a bad toupee and thick black sunglasses, smiled and pulled a silver lighter from a pocket. The workman leaned forward into the flame, puffed and stepped back. After they'd exchanged a few more words, the man in green returned to his partner.

''How many men do you need, Ironman?'' Price asked.

Lyons felt his fingers tighten around the phone. The whole little minidrama in the hall had all looked innocent. Too innocent? Or was his imagination working overtime after the incident in the General Assembly room?

Price cleared her throat in his ear. ''Ironman, are you listening? I asked you how many men you wanted.''

Lyons continued to stare down the hall. ''Send me at least two dozen,'' he said, then paused, thinking. ''Dress them in gray suits so they'll blend in around here. But have them all wear a clashing tie. That should do it.''

Price's laugh was more from tension than mirth. "Maybe I should consult Gadgets on the fashion end. There's nobody better at wearing things that clash."

Lyons didn't laugh. He watched the green-clad workmen continue down the hall to the corner and disappear. "Sorry Barbara," he said into the phone. "My sense of humor has been temporarily misplaced on the floor of the General Assembly hall."

Always the professional, Price said, "I understand. How soon do you want the reinforcements?"

Lyons watched the man in the toupee nod to the others. The South Americans turned and strode purposely down the hall to the same corner the workmen had turned. "I needed them ten minutes ago," the ex-cop said into the phone and hung up.

He cradled the phone, stood and opened the door. He started down the hall, the tension creeping back into his gut as the South Americans disappeared around the corner.

Lyons had broken into a jog by the time the first shot rang out.

BARBARA PRICE DROPPED the phone into the cradle, an uneasy feeling creeping through her. Carl "Ironman" Lyons had gotten his nickname for good reason. The ex-LAPD detective seemed to be made of iron; not just his steel-hard muscular body, his emotions as well.

But Stony Man Farm's mission controller knew the Able Team leader well, and she knew that beneath the iron exterior, he was flesh and blood. He had feelings, emotions, loves and hates.

Price lifted the phone again and swiveled in her chair, looking through the plate-glass wall that separated Mission Control and Communications from the computer room. High atop his work ramp, where in one quick glance he could take in the multitude of computer screens, disk drives, Teletypes and other equipment Price couldn't even name, sat Aaron "The Bear" Kurtzman.

Wild hair curled down Kurtzman's neck and over his ears. He stared intently at the screen in front of his wheelchair, his forehead glowing under the lights with its customary film of sweat. Price watched the man's lips move as he whispered something to himself, his fingers streaking across the computer keyboard like some maestro pianist.

Price smiled as she punched his intercom extension. Kurtzman was a master with his magic machines, and had the same finesse with his instruments as a most accomplished musician. Through the glass she watched him scowl as the buzzer broke his concentration. He reached for the phone with his left hand, his right never slowing down as it continued to peck away at the keys.

"Yeah, Barb?"

"Ironman needs two dozen more men. Who have we got available?"

Kurtzman sighed. "How quick you need this, Barb? I'm right in the middle of—"

"He said ten minutes ago, Aaron."

Kurtzman's hand finally stopped typing. He turned toward the window. Price saw the concern register on his face. He kept the receiver against his ear as he pushed a button on his armrest. The wheelchair spun 180 degrees. "Let me pull it up on this other screen," he said.

"Sure."

He tapped the keys on the other computer, then sat back and crossed his arms. Five seconds later, he nodded and said, "Here's the list. I'm sending it your way. Anything else?"

"No, Aaron. Thanks."

Kurtzman smiled into the glass, then turned his chair around and hung up.

A moment later, the laser printer on the table next to Price's console clicked on. A hard copy of the Stony Man troops not currently on assignment came sliding out the side.

Price grabbed a pencil. She frowned as she went down the list, passing by some of the names, making a check mark in the margin by others. When she'd picked twenty-four men, she lifted the phone again and punched the number for John "The Cowboy" Kissinger in the Stony Man armory.

"Get some firepower ready, Cowboy," she said. "Something that can hide under gray pinstripes."

"How many men?" Kissinger asked.

"Two dozen."

"Roger," Kissinger said and hung up.

Price held the button down, got another dial tone and lifted the list. She punched the number for Personnel and read the twenty-four names into the receiver. "Have them ready to pull out in ten minutes."

She sat back, took a deep breath, then smiled as she lifted the phone again. Gray suits and clashing ties, Lyons had said.

Okay, it was time for the hard part.

Almost *any* color went with gray.

BOLAN DARTED PAST Goran Englebretson to the front window. Six more North Haakovian army jeeps pulled to a halt in the front yard. Behind him, the Executioner heard the resistance men scrambling for the weapons scattered around the room. He turned back as Englebretson struggled unsteadily to his feet.

The old man rubbed his legs and grimaced.

"Can you run?" Bolan asked.

Englebretson shook his head. "My legs are old. Arthritic." He stamped the floor gingerly and pain shot through his face again. "But there is no need to run," he said, forcing a smile.

Bolan glanced through the window into the darkness. The shadowy forms of soldiers armed with Kalashnikovs and Danuvia subguns were exiting the jeeps. Several walked toward the vehicles already parked in the yard.

In seconds they would discover the drivers who had fallen to the Executioner's first wave of attack.

The warrior hurried to Englebretson. "There's a good twenty, twenty-five men out there. Not good odds." He glanced down at the frail man. "I can carry you—"

Englebretson chuckled and pointed behind the Executioner, who turned to see that two of the men had moved a table to the side of the room. Another was rolling back a throw rug.

A trapdoor appeared in the wooden floor.

Through the window, Bolan heard one of the soldiers shout. Excited voices joined in.

A resistance man wearing a black leather driving cap yanked open the trapdoor, and he and another man ducked out of sight.

Englebretson turned to a tall slender man who was rocking back and forth from his heels to the balls of his feet. "Erik, as soon as we have closed the door, replace the carpet and table."

The man nodded, then spread his legs and leaned onto one knee, stretching.

Bolan frowned.

Englebretson started down the steps into the hole. "Do not worry, Pollock," he said over his shoulder. "I might not be able to run. But Erik is here."

The Executioner started down the steps behind him. "Hope he's fast." He turned, grabbed the trapdoor and lowered it. Suddenly he found himself in total darkness.

A small penlight flickered below him. Ten feet farther down, he saw Englebretson kneeling painfully at the bottom of the steps. The freedom fighter called out softly to the other men, out of sight somewhere along the tunnel. "Go on," he said. "Pollock and I will catch up."

The Executioner moved cautiously down the stairs, hearing the wood creak with every step. He knelt on the cool damp earth next to Englebretson.

The old man held the flashlight under his chin, illuminating his face. The folds and wrinkles around his eyes took on a weird orange glow. "Follow me," he whispered, "and try not to bump the ceiling. We had no time to reinforce it, and it could cave in any second."

Bolan glanced over his head. Dust trickled down into his eyes.

Englebretson turned and started down the narrow passageway on hands and knees. He began to gasp for air after the first fifteen feet.

The Executioner slowed his pace. He had seen all brands of courage during the years he'd fought the evil of the world, and he respected them all. But most of the men he had seen perform acts of bravery had been young, strong and in good shape.

Englebretson was none of these. The old man's bones and muscles ached with every movement, and unless Bolan missed his guess, Goran Englebretson's lungs had fallen victim to years in the North Haakovian coal mines. Yet the dedicated man didn't give up the fight. Nor did he complain. He continued his war against the diabolic despot who ruled his homeland, fighting toe-to-toe with men young enough to be his grandsons.

That took courage, all right. A special kind of courage. But even more than courage, it took dedication, commitment.

Five minutes later, the tunnel widened. Englebretson rolled to a sitting position, stared at the ceiling and gasped for air. He held his hand up, indicating that he needed a moment, then pointed overhead with the flashlight and said, "We ... are ... here."

Bolan looked up to see another trapdoor, which was slightly ajar. He rose to a crouch and lifted the lid. A hand shot down through the opening he'd created. The man in the black leather driving cap pulled him out into the night.

The Executioner's eyes skirted the area as he reached down, grasping Englebretson's frail arm. The tunnel opened in the dirt next to a chicken-wire fence that separated a block of houses from a gravel-covered alley. Somewhere behind him, a cat shrieked and then a trash-can lid clattered to the pebbles.

Bolan pulled Englebretson through the hole and to his feet. He crouched, yanking the Desert Eagle from his holster as running footsteps echoed down the alley. Turning, he saw Erik slow to a halt. A grin covered the runner's face. His breathing was barely above normal.

Englebretson's lungs heaved like a billow as a freedom fighter in a gray *shrapki* and matching overcoat grabbed one of his arms. Erik helped steady his leader by the shoulders.

"Are you all right?" the man in the black cap whispered.

"Of course," Englebretson gasped. He looked contemptuously at the hands on his body, then shrugged them off. "Is it you two or me who needs help?"

Bolan couldn't suppress a smile.

Englebretson hacked, spit phlegm onto the ground, then turned back to Erik. "Cover the hole," he ordered, and the thin man began scooping dirt over the trapdoor with his hands.

The resistance leader paused. "No, on second thought," he said, "Stensvik's men will find the tunnel soon, anyway. We cannot use the safehouse again." His eyes fell on the Executioner's battle harness. "May we use one of your..." His voice trailed off as if he were trying to think of the English word he wanted.

Bolan nodded. "You may." He jerked one of the frag grenades hanging from his harness, and it dropped into his hand. Erik reopened the trap and the Executioner pulled the pin.

Holding the clamp together in his fist, Bolan leaned into the hole. He propelled the grenade as far into the darkness as he could, and heard it bounce along the soft earth as he rose and slammed the lid over the opening.

A second later, the earth rumbled softly beneath their feet.

The man in the black leather cap led them silently down the alley, then through a gate into a backyard. Hens clucked and unseen wings fluttered in the night as they moved past a chicken coop to the back door of a small one-story dwelling.

The man in the rabbit hat moved forward and rapped lightly on the weathered back door.

A few moments later, the door cracked open. Long blond hair fell through the opening, then an emerald green eye appeared to inspect them.

The door swung open, and Bolan followed Englebretson and his men inside.

A tall, willowy shadow lighted a candle and led them down the hall to a kitchen. As the woman turned back to them, Bolan looked above the flame to see the mate to the eye that had gazed through the doorway. Long locks of white blond hair fell down the woman's neck past her shoulders, almost to her waist. She looked at the Executioner briefly, her cream-colored skin glowing softly in the candlelight, then turned and placed the candle holder on the kitchen table. When she twisted back again, the light behind her crept through the light cotton nightgown, outlining the soft feminine curves of her body.

The effect was dazzling. A sexual yet innocent allure oozed from every pore of the woman's body, and the Executioner saw the other men fighting the urge to stare through the gown.

Bolan felt the muscles in his groin tighten involuntarily, and looked away. The woman was beautiful, there was no denying it. But she was obviously the wife or girlfriend of one of the young freedom fighters. It wouldn't do to stare.

Englebretson took a seat at one end of the kitchen table, Bolan dropped into a rickety chair at the other and the rest of the men found places between them on both sides. The woman moved automatically to the stove, and a moment later the aroma of coffee filtered through the air.

Like the flashlight had done in the tunnel, the candle now illuminated Englebretson's face, emphasizing both the wrinkles and the pain behind his cool black eyes. The flame flickered and sent ghostly, oversize shadows of the men's heads and shoulders dancing across the cracked wallpaper.

"First," Englebretson whispered, "let me thank you again."

Bolan shook his head. "No need."

The old man nodded. "I see you are not a man to bask in your own glory. That is good. Then we will get down to business. I understand you have come on a recon mission. You wish to see potential bombing locations. For when the war begins again?"

Bolan nodded.

The woman circled the table, setting coffee mugs in front of each of the men. "*If* the war begins again," she said. "Perhaps it will not—"

Englebretson smiled wearily, the years on his face doubling with the effort. "It will," he said simply.

The man in the leather cap nodded. "For us, it has never stopped."

The woman returned to the stove, lifted the coffeepot and began filling their cups. As she leaned over next to Bolan, light wisps of hair brushed across his cheek.

The Executioner glanced up. The startling green eyes stared innocently at his coffee cup as it filled. She moved on.

Englebretson spoke again. "We will show you the sites we feel most vulnerable to air attack," he said, "and we will show you other locations that could be taken out from the ground. We will trade intelligence, and all of our meager resources will be open to you." He stared blankly at the Executioner "In fact I have but one thing I will not share with you." He stopped as the woman bent to fill his cup.

Bolan's eyes narrowed. If they were to work together, they had to trust each other completely. They had to be a team, sharing everything. And it would be best to get any problems out in the open right away, before the bullets started flying. "What's that?" the Executioner asked.

Englebretson's smile returned, but this time instead of accenting his age, a twinkle gleamed in his eyes. The wrinkles road-mapping his weathered face seemed to smooth out, and he suddenly looked twenty years younger. As the beautiful blond woman straightened next to him, he slipped an arm around her waist.

She turned toward him, her face lighting up with love.

Englebretson patted the woman's waist. "My wife," he said chuckling. "Ingmarie."

The woman bent again and kissed him long and full on the lips.

Bolan raised his coffee cup and smiled. "Okay. That's fair enough."

Englebretson broke away from his wife's embrace and the kiss looked as if it had taken another twenty years off his age. He turned back to Bolan, his face a mask of pride. "As they say in America," he said. "Not bad for..." He paused, frowning, again trying to find the correct word.

Then his eyes sparkled again. He laughed. "Not too bad for such an old fart, eh?"

THE MAN BEHIND THE DESK in the Oval Office was surprised the call hadn't come sooner.

"Yes, President Hugosson," he said into the phone. "What can I do for you today, sir?"

The Finnish leader cleared his throat. "You were behind the infiltration of my southern border," he said. It was a simple statement of fact, rather than an accusation.

The President played his part. "I'm sorry, Mr. Hugosson, I'm afraid I don't know what you're talking about."

There was a long pause. "It could only have been Americans," the Finnish leader said. "They infiltrated my country without injuring any of my men. No one else would have gone to such trouble or risk."

"Mr. Hugosson," the Man said, "I still don't understand what you're talking—"

Hugosson sighed. "Let us dispense with the charade. You have made your point," he said. "I will tighten security on all borders."

"Evidently, Mr. Hugosson," he said, "something of which I am unaware has happened to make you realize the extent of the North Haakovia threat. Am I correct?"

Hugosson sighed again. "Since you insist on continuing this little game, I will play along. You are correct. I understand the threat."

"Then may I assume you will reconsider allowing the U.S. to send troops into southern Finland? As a precautionary backup measure?"

The Finnish leader had been ready for this one. "No. That will not be necessary. Our military is quite up to the challenge. And let me assure you, Mr. President, any American troops found on Finnish soil will be considered terrorists. And dealt with accordingly."

5

There was something incongruous about Helsinki, something that Yakov Katzenelenbogen had never been able to put his finger on. But the city never failed to overwhelm him, and each time he visited the capital of Finland, he was filled with two emotions.

The beauty of Helsinki's construction took his breath away.

And this undefined inconsistency perplexed him.

The Phoenix Force leader stared down from the top of the Olympic Stadium Tower to the main post office and railway station in the center of the city. From his vantage point it was like looking at an architect's miniature model of a projected building project. The thin line that was actually four-lane Mannerheimintie Street started in Helsinki's central hub and ran past him, all the way to the main Turku road to his rear. Scattered along the route, Katz could see the house of parliament, Finlandia Hall, the air terminal and a dozen other points of interest to tourists.

The aging Israeli sighed under his breath. For the past four hundred years the builders of Helsinki, from King Gustav Vasa of Sweden to the present, had wasted no space. An incredible amount of first-class architecture was crammed into the relatively small area of peninsulas, bays and islands that made up the city.

But still, somehow, the builders had found space for the green parks and broad streets that also met Katz's gaze, and as he stared through the dusk that had fallen over the city, Katzenelenbogen suddenly realized that it was this dichotomy that made the city appear contradictory, paradoxical.

Helsinki was crowded . . . yet spacious.

The Israeli breathed in, letting the clean, crisp Scandinavian air fill his lungs. Below, no matter which direction he looked, the city looked peaceful. A surge of tension shot through his chest as another contradiction worked its way from his unconscious mind to conscious thought.

Yes. A peaceful city. Except for the fact that Dag Vaino was somewhere below.

Katz felt a tap on his arm. He turned to see Calvin James. Like himself and the rest of Phoenix Force, James wore blue jeans, athletic shoes and a sweatshirt—the former Navy SEAL's shirt bearing the logo of the Chicago Bears. Katz had questioned the wisdom of this manner of dress, but Barbara Price had done her homework. She had convinced him that American football was the current fashion rage all over Scandinavia, and that only by dressing like Americans could they appear to be natives.

Another contradiction.

The Israeli studied James as the black Phoenix Force warrior gazed over the guardrail through a pair of binoculars. James had added a long, loose, leather trench coat to his ensemble for two reasons: first, it kept out the biting Finnish wind. But it also hid the Uzi submachine gun and other weapons that hung from his shoulders.

James's face tightened behind the binoculars. "I think I see it."

"The house?"

"No, too far away. But I'm pretty sure it's the right street. Price did say Appollonk, didn't she?"

Katz nodded, then glanced at his wrist. "Let's go, then. McCarter and Manning should be back any minute with the car."

James followed him to the elevator, and they rode down. Rafael Encizo still waited at the stadium's front steps. The little Cuban wore a black waist-length Los Angeles Raiders starter jacket. He gripped the neck of a Three Towers beer bottle in one hand.

James grinned and shook his head as they neared. "You drink like a *pescado,* Pescado."

Encizo glanced at the bottle and laughed. "It's what they call Class III beer over here, smart-ass," he said. "Near beer. You might be able to get a buzz off it, but you'd have to chug about two hundred bottles."

A navy Volvo station wagon pulled to a halt in front of the steps. Katz glanced in to see David McCarter behind the wheel, his red University of Oklahoma sweater rolled up over his forearms. Gary Manning, clad in a similar OU parka with Sooners emblazoned across the front, rode shotgun.

James opened the door and the three men climbed in back.

"Any problem at the rental office?" Katz asked.

McCarter shook his head. "No, but the bloke behind the counter wanted to buy my jacket from me."

Twenty minutes later, the Volvo turned off Tookankatu Avenue onto Museokatu, then cut south into an area of modern apartment buildings and town houses. Katz watched through the window as McCarter drove slowly past the house Price had fingered through Kurtzman's link into CIA files. One-story, frame duplex. That meant three sides, three paths of escape—front and back doors, side windows. A new Toyota and older Datsun sedan were parked in the driveway.

"How current is this intel Kurtzman picked up?" Manning asked from the front seat.

"Yesterday afternoon," Katz replied. "The Company got it through Mossad."

"Oh, then it's *bound* to be accurate," McCarter said dryly.

Katz grinned and went on. "Vaino's supposed to have come here right after the Varkaus assassination." He leaned forward and tapped McCarter on the shoulder. "Drive another block down and kill the lights. You and I will go to the front. Cal take the rear. Rafe, you and Gary cover the side windows, then come in. One of you through the front, the other take the back."

Four heads nodded agreement as McCarter pulled the Volvo to a stop in the parking lot of an apartment complex.

Katz got out quietly, walked to the rear of the station wagon and opened the door. A stack of green plastic trash bags rested just inside, and one by one he lifted their oblong shapes and handed them to the rest of the men. As the men of Phoenix Force waited, he slipped a pair of blue-striped coveralls over his clothes, then picked up a large metal tool box.

Phoenix Force started up the street toward the house where Dag Vaino waited.

A half block away, James broke from the party and disappeared between another pair of duplex apartments. As they reached the duplex next door, Encizo and Manning angled toward the two windows on the side of the safehouse while Katz and McCarter marched boldly up the sidewalk to the front porch.

Katz reached for the doorbell, while McCarter took up position to the side, out of sight. As the Phoenix Force leader pressed the button, the Briton ripped the plastic bag from his 9 mm Sten Mark II submachine gun.

The bell chimed inside the house. A moment later, feet padded toward the door. "Who is it?" a voice called out in Finnish.

Yakov Katzenelenbogen had done his homework. He'd learned the Finnish word for "repairman," and now shouted it through the barrier.

There was a long pause, then the voice inside said, "Who sent you?"

Katz flipped the catch on the toolbox and reached inside. "The Angel of Death," he answered in Hebrew and kicked in the door.

The tiny Belgian-made Steyr machine pistol jumped from the toolbox to his hand as the door swung open, knocking a dark figure back into the shadows. Katz let the box fall from his false arm, clattering to the concrete porch as he stepped into the house. His good hand streaked for the wall, found the switch and flipped it up, bathing the entryway in light. He heard the splinter of wood somewhere at the rear of the building, and then the familiar rat-ta-ta-tat of Calvin James's Uzi.

The man who had answered the door sat stunned on the floor, his forehead beginning to swell where the door had hit him. He came suddenly to his senses, and his hand darted under his shirt to his waistband.

Katz stepped forward, catching him under the chin with a front snap kick and slamming him up and back into the wall.

A 9 mm Makarov automatic clanked to the tile of the entryway. The man's eyes closed and he slumped to the floor.

Gunfire continued from the other rooms of the house. Katz heard McCarter enter behind him, and at the same time saw a flash of blue in the door to the living room. He turned, raising the machine pistol to chest-level and pulling the trigger.

A burst of 5.7 mm hollowpoints sailed from the barrel of the compact Steyr, cutting through the denim jacket of a blond-bearded man trying to bring an AK-47 into play.

The Israeli heard more rapid fire behind him as McCarter's Sten added a volley of 9 mm slugs to the denim jacket.

Katz moved cautiously to the door, dropped to one knee against the wall and peered around the corner into the living room. Two men had attempted to conceal themselves behind a couch. The barrels of their assault rifles extended over the top toward the entryway. To their left, behind an overturned table, two legs extended from the sides of the barrier.

Two different pant legs. Two more men. The table had been set at an angle so they could cover both the entryway and a door in the far wall.

A shot came from the rear of the house, then both men rose to fire into the far doorway.

At the same time bullets from behind the couch sailed past Katz's nose. He jerked back.

The Israeli rose to his feet and stepped back from the wall. The little 5.7 mm rounds his one-handed machine pistol spit might not be large, but they had terrific penetration. Turning briefly to McCarter, he said, "Cover me," then dropped the magazine from the Steyr. Reaching under his jacket, he produced an extra mag filled with needle-tipped armor-piercing slugs, and rammed it up the butt of the machine pistol.

He took a deep breath, frowning in concentration as he stared at the wall and estimated the angle toward the couch. Then, raising the Steyr to shoulder-level, he squeezed the trigger, swinging the Steyr back and forth in figure eights, blanketing the wall with rounds. Tiny holes appeared in the wall, growing larger as the Steyr continued to sputter. White dust rained through the air as the rounds gradually stripped the wallboard from the studs.

Finally the Steyr's slide blew back and locked open. Katz slammed another magazine of armor-piercing steel jackets into the weapon. He stepped up to the wall and peered through one of the gaping holes.

Pieces of upholstery and splinters of wood littered the living room. The gun barrels that had been behind the couch now lay on the floor.

Movement to their rear caused both Phoenix Force warriors to spin, their weapons ready.

Rafael Encizo stepped into the house.

Another Uzi chattered from the back of the house, which generated return fire from behind the overturned table. Katz stuck the Steyr through the wall.

A half mag of 5.7 mm rounds sailed through the wall into the table, drilling through the cheap pressed wood.

A sudden scream of desperation came from behind the barrier, then a gunman wearing a slick black leather jacket leaped to his feet and sprinted toward the entryway. Terrified eyes blazed panic as the rifle in his hands jumped wildly.

Katz and McCarter answered the assault, both warriors sending short choppy bursts from their weapons into the face and leather jacket of the terrorist.

The house went suddenly silent.

McCarter caught Katz's attention and nodded toward the door. Katz nodded back, reading his mind. The Israeli moved to the opening as the Briton drew in a breath, then dived into the living room and rolled to the couch.

McCarter looked back to the doorway and shook his head.

"James!" Katz shouted.

"Back here!"

"Manning?"

A small series of taps sounded on the glass from outside the window.

Katz led the way cautiously into the living room. He joined McCarter behind the couch and looked down at the floor. Two terrorists lay dead, their tattered bodies still leaking blood.

But neither bore the face of Dag Vaino.

The Phoenix Force leader moved on to the table. The body count grew by two, but neither of the men fit Vaino's description.

James stepped cautiously into the room from the kitchen, his Uzi at the ready.

"How many back there?" Katz asked.

"Four. All dead."

"Any of them Vaino?"

The former SEAL shook his head.

Footsteps sounded in the kitchen, and four assault weapons rose to cover the door.

Manning stepped into the living room and the guns lowered. "Vaino's not here?"

Katz shook his head.

Manning snorted in disgust. "Back to the old drawing board."

"Maybe not," Katz growled. He spun on his heel and stalked back to the entryway. Kneeling by the terrorist he'd kicked upon entering the house, he slapped the man's face gently, then harder when he got no response.

Finally the man's eyes opened.

"Where's Vaino?" the Israeli demanded. "We know he was here. How'd he get out?"

The dark eyes in the round Slavic skull flickered right and left. Then the terrorist's lips curled up in contempt. "If you think I will tell you that, you are in for a long night."

Katz looked up. "Cal."

James stepped forward and lifted the tail of his Chicago Bears sweatshirt. From the sheath stuck in his belt he drew a stainless-steel, six-inch blade.

The Phoenix Force warrior knelt next to Katz and pressed the edge of the knife against the terrorist's throat. "It might be a long night for us, dude," he said. "But for you, it's gonna seem like eternity." It took little intimidation for the man to yield an address—148 Rolfe.

LYONS BROKE INTO A SPRINT as the shot echoed around the corner and down the hall. The Colt Python .357 filled his hand, the spongy Pachmayer grips nestling into the web between his thumb and index finger.

The Able Team leader hit the tile twenty feet from the corner, landing on his side as if he were sliding into third base. He slid past the wall and felt the air heat up against his cheek as a volley of fire sailed past his head.

Lyons's eyes took in the situation as he slowed in the middle of the cross hall. The "Peruvians" had produced automatic weapons from the boxes borne by the "workmen." Joined by the workmen themselves, they now fired toward the row of South African busts farther down the hall.

Blancanales, Baker and Karns had crowded three South Haakovian delegates behind the marble stands that supported the iron figureheads. Blancanales had taken refuge behind a bust of President de Klerk, and a burst of 7.62 mm rounds streaked toward him, clanging tinnily off the iron bust.

Lyons slid to a halt in the middle of the hall, then rolled to his side to get Pol, the agents and South Haakovians out of his line of fire. One of the green-clad workmen cut loose with the Kalashnikov, sending a burst into the iron statues.

Fixing the Python's front ramp sight on the man's back, Lyons drilled a round into his spine. The Russian assault rifle tumbled out of his hands, and the would-be assassin doubled over as he lost control of his arms and legs.

Blancanales snapped a 9 mm parabellum into the chest of another workman. His Uzi clattered to the floor, and he sprawled next to his comrade.

Lyons pulled the trigger again, and one of the "Peruvians" fell. The ex-cop's third .357 round drilled a bald man with a thick mustache. The force spun the killer, and a fourth round from the Python gouged into his throat, nearly severing his head from his shoulders.

Secret Service Agent Tom Karns's head appeared between effigies of Lords Roberts and Kitchener. The agent started to shoot, then Lyons saw him hesitate. From the corner of his eye the ex-cop noticed a flurry of movement as two light-complected men in business suits walked into the hall.

The men's mouths fell open, as they froze in their tracks.

Directly in Karns's line of fire.

Gunfire continued to explode around them, but Lyons had no time to wonder what kind of fools would walk toward the obvious noise. Vaulting to his feet, he lunged toward the men, his cross-body block catching the closer man across the knees.

The man tumbled against his partner, and all three men fell to the floor in a flurry of arms and legs.

"Stay down!" Lyons ordered. He turned back to the melee in time to see Karns double-action the first shot from his SIG-Sauer P-220, then follow up with two single-action 9 mm slugs. All three rounds went into the gut of a false Peruvian wearing a blue pin-striped suit.

But the interference of the Swedes had given the man the time he needed. Even as Karns's rounds struck home, he pulled the trigger of his Ingram

MAC-10 and sent a volley of 9 mm rounds streaking into the Secret Service man's head.

Karns toppled from behind the busts, dead before he hit the tile.

Lyons felt the bile rise in his stomach as he rose to one knee, gripping the Python in his right hand. As he squeezed the trigger, his left hand shot under his coat to the small of his back for the sound-suppressed Government Model .45.

The .357 round caught a phony diplomat in the back of the head. The man's skull exploded, and he joined the growing mass of bloody bodies sprawled on the hall floor of the General Assembly building.

Baker's head appeared above the iron figure of Lord Methuen. The Secret Service agent stroked the trigger of a stainless-steel Smith & Wesson Model 66. The two-and-a-half-inch barrel jumped toward the ceiling with the recoil, but the bullet sailed true, catching the last would-be killer square between the eyes.

The gunfire suddenly stopped, but the echo resounding off the walls continued to buzz in Carl Lyons's head as if he'd rung the bells of Notre Dame with no ear protectors. Hurrying toward the busts, he saw Tom Karns on the floor.

The South Haakovian diplomats lay huddled in a frightened mass behind the marble platforms. They looked up with fearful eyes.

A dozen more Secret Service men hurried down the hall from both ends. They stopped, forming a protective circle around the diplomats.

Blancanales raced to Lyons's side. He indicated the assassins with his Beretta. "Who were these guys?" he asked. "They don't look Haakovian."

Lyons shrugged, the remorse he'd felt over Karns's death suddenly becoming anger. "I don't know. Cubans, maybe. Or Arab terrorists Stensvik hired." He stopped and drew a deep breath. "But I've taken about all of this I can stand, Pol. We might not know now who they are, but we're damn sure about to find out."

The Able Team leader elbowed his way through the ring of Secret Service agents and looked down at the men on the floor. Several briefcases lay scattered among the throng. Without asking, the ex-cop lifted the closest one and opened it.

"What are you doing?" one of the South Haakovians demanded. "That belongs to me. Give it—"

Lyons ignored him. He ripped several sheets of white typing paper from the briefcase and dropped it on the man. "There," he said. Then hurrying to where the attackers lay, he knelt next to the man in the blue pin-striped suit. Pulling a cheap ballpoint pen from his pocket, he broke it in half and let the ink drip to the tile.

The Able Team leader rolled the body over, for the first time noticing the strange tattoo on the forearm. An angel, fiery red eyes blazing with vengeance, swooped down from the heavens brandishing a broadsword. Quickly the ex-cop pressed the still-warm fingers into the pool of ink, then rolled them across one of the sheets of typing paper. He wrote "tattoo" across the top of the page, then moved to the next man.

Lyons repeated the process on the two other men who'd masqueraded as Peruvians. He wrote "facial scar" and "blue pinstripe" at the top of the pages for future identification. The phony workmen came last, and he designated them simply with "short" and "tall."

Gadgets Schwarz appeared next to him, saw what he was doing and hurried away. The Able Team electronics man came back a moment later carrying a small case. Lyons rose and the two men hurried down the hall as the Secret Service began herding the diplomats to safety. Seeing an empty conference room, they ducked inside.

Gadgets found an electrical outlet, set the portable fax on the conference table and plugged it into the wall. A few minutes later, the fingerprints of the five men disguised as Peruvian diplomats and workmen were flying over the lines to Stony Man Farm.

The Able Team leader took a seat at the table and stared at the wall, the fury in his soul mounting and threatening to take control. What the President had ordered them to do was impossible. For full protection the Haakovians needed to be isolated and under guard, not running free through the General Assembly building. Tom Karns had died trying to follow these incredible orders, and it was a miracle there hadn't been more deaths.

It was a miracle that all of them, including the South Haakovian delegation, weren't lying in a massive river of blood right now.

The ex-cop's fingers dug into the edge of the table as he awaited the response from Stony Man. Able Team was used to stacked odds and suicide assignments. It was part of their job description.

But what about the other men risking their lives here at the UN? What about the Secret Service, the individual bodyguard teams and the regular UN guards? None of them, not even the Secret Service, had the high level of training and experience that he, Pol and Gadgets enjoyed. Was it fair to them?

What about Tom Karns, dammit? Karns had died not for his country, or anybody else's country. He had died for politics.

The fax clicked into action. Lyons rose and walked to the machine, taking a position next to Gadgets. The first paragraph concerned the "tall" and "short" men disguised in green work clothes. It said simply, "No Record."

But Stony Man Farm had had better luck with the phony Peruvian diplomats. Their fingerprints had been classified, and Lyons read the names and descriptions next to the classifications as they rolled out of the printer:

Gonzales, Fredrico Alonzo
DOB: 11-21-55. 5'7". 180 lbs. Brown. Brown.
Tattoo right forearm: Angel with sword.

Lopez, Pedro Simon
DOB: 4-4-49. 5′9″. 148 lbs. Black. Brown. Knife
scar, left cheek.

Guttierez, Emmanuel Rosca
DOB: 1-15-52. Black. Brown. No visible distinguishing marks.

The printer stopped momentarily, then started again. Lyons felt the anger return to his chest as a short, simple conclusion appeared at the end of the fax page. The ex-cop's fingers curled into fists as he read the words.

As he'd believed all along, Able Team was being wasted. The Secret Service was more than capable of protecting the Haakovians—provided the diplomats consented to a lower profile. And Stensvik's operation was far more complex than the President imagined. There were elements to the mystery of which the Man wasn't aware, pieces of the puzzle Able Team could be, *should be,* running down and putting together.

One such piece now stared Carl Lyons in the face. He blinked, then reread the words Barbara Price had added at the end of the fingerprint IDs. *All three suspects believed to be in the employ of the Medellín drug cartel.*

Gadgets shook his head. "And here we are baby-sitting, Ironman."

Lyons turned and started for the door. "Yeah, but not for long, Gadgets. Not for long."

INGMARIE AND ERIK disappeared from the room. When they returned a moment later, the woman wore a heavy blue wool sweater and skirt. She threw an equally thick topcoat over her shoulders and hid her blond hair under a black stocking cap.

Erik wore the white uniform of a North Haakovian navy ensign.

"Ready?" Englebretson asked.

Bolan nodded.

Ingmarie on his arm, Englebretson led the way out of the house. Erik, Hans—the man in the rabbit coat and hat—and Bolan followed him to the garage a few feet away. The hinges on the overhead door screamed for oil as Erik opened it to reveal a rusty Chevrolet van.

"Hans, you drive," Englebretson ordered. Erik took the shotgun seat while Bolan, Ingmarie and the aging guerrilla leader slipped into the back.

Twenty minutes later, they passed through a small gulf-side village. The lights of North Haakovia's Lenin naval base appeared in the distance. Hans pulled the van into the thick trees alongside the road and killed the lights. A mile or so ahead, the Executioner could see the guard shack of a minor entrance gate. Two tiny figures stood inside the glass. A twenty-foot chain-link fence topped with razor wire ran out of sight into the trees on both sides of the gate.

Englebretson leaned over and kissed his wife. "Be careful, darling."

Ingmarie nodded. She and Erik exited the vehicle and crept through the trees toward the gate.

Bolan followed Englebretson and Hans out of the van and deeper into the woods. They slipped quietly toward the base.

A half hour later they peered through the dense foliage to see the fence sparkling under the perimeter lights. Angling back toward the road, they crept through the trees until the gate appeared.

Bolan peered through the limbs. Suddenly, from the road behind them, a shrill female shriek broke the still night.

The guards swiveled toward the noise, unslinging their AK-74s.

Another shriek. Then the words, "No! Please! No!"

Bolan watched Ingmarie stagger from the woods to the road. Her sweater had been ripped to the waist. Deep scratches on her breasts were visible under the approach lights, and her face was red in several places, as if she'd been slapped.

Erik, dressed in the clearly visible white uniform, appeared briefly on the road, looked up at the guard shack, then turned and sprinted away into the trees.

"Please! Help me!" Ingmarie screamed, then collapsed to the ground.

One of the guards, a short stocky man, left the shack. He waddled to where the woman lay and knelt at her side. Then, turning back, he laughed and called out to his partner in Haakovian.

Englebretson translated, his jaw grinding in hatred as he whispered. "He told the other man not to get excited. It is just one of their boys having a little fun with a town slut." The freedom fighter turned to the Executioner. "They will try to rape her themselves, now. It is always the same. Stensvik and his men take what they want."

Englebretson turned toward the road but continued to whisper. "This *must* be done," he said as if trying harder to convince himself than Bolan. "But I never grow accustomed to some of the sacrifices we must make for freedom. Let's go."

Bolan joined the freedom fighters as they crept along the fence beneath the line of sight of the guard in the shack. As they neared the open door, they heard the man shout down the road. "Bring her here, Fedor! I am due for a break, and could use a little of that myself!" He cackled in anticipation.

As the man on the road reached down and hauled Ingmarie to her feet, Bolan reached through the door and jerked the guard from the shack.

A right cross from the Executioner wiped the surprised expression from the man's face.

The warrior turned back to the road. The guard gripped Ingmarie's shoulder with one hand while the other groped her breasts. The woman whimpered in protest, and the guard threw back his head and laughed.

Ingmarie reached suddenly under her skirt and drew a stiletto. Twisting, she drove the blade up and into the man's thick throat.

The guard's laughter turned to raspy coughs as blood shot from his neck. Then he stared blankly into the night for a moment before falling forward onto his face.

Erik appeared again. He and Ingmarie dragged the body into the trees.

At the guard shack Hans had already begun to remove the other guard's uniform. He dressed quickly as Bolan stuffed the body out of view.

Erik and Ingmarie hurried back from the trees. Erik had traded his ensign uniform for that of the man Ingmarie had stabbed. He took his place next to Hans inside the shack, found a thermos of ice water and went to work removing the blood that covered the front of the shirt.

Hans grinned. "Comrades," he said to Bolan, Englebretson and Ingmarie, "your papers are in order." He waved them through.

An all-terrain vehicle marked Security stood just inside the gate, and Englebretson slid behind the wheel. Bolan took the seat next to him as Ingmarie got in back. The old man drove slowly toward the docks, pointing out possible bombing sites. "The armory," he said as they passed a fortified concrete bunker.

Enlisted men hurried in and out of the building, carrying boxes of various size and shape to a line of supply trucks parked in front of the armory. Even in the cold night, sweat poured from their foreheads and there was an atmosphere of urgency about their movements.

Bolan and the freedom fighters passed a four-story dormitory. "Top three floors are officers' quarters," Englebretson remarked. "Ground floor, offices."

The lights in most of the windows were on. Behind a set of open curtains on the first floor, the Executioner saw several men in full uniform seated around a conference table. Another man stood, his finger jabbing excitedly at a map on the wall as he spoke. Again, the Executioner noted the ambience of gravity in the man's actions.

As they drove on through the base, it became more and more obvious.

North Haakovia was in the last phase of preparing for war.

Bolan clicked away with his camera, also making mental notes of each site, confident that he'd be able to draw the pilots a map when he returned to Larsborg.

"Of course the main bombing sites will be along the water," Englebretson said as they neared the docks. "Gunships, aircraft carriers, even nuclear submarines are always anchored here." They turned and drove parallel to the water, passing several of the vessels the freedom fighter had named. The Executioner continued to record it on film.

Bolan frowned as a freighter suddenly appeared in the distance. As they neared, the flying colors of Norway became visible above the main mast. At least two dozen armed men stood guard around the ship as more men carried crates down a gangway. Still others carried crates from the dock onto the deck.

"They're loading and unloading," Bolan said. "Any idea what it is?"

Englebretson frowned. "No, but I have never seen that many guards for a freighter. For that matter, why is a Norwegian freighter at a naval base to begin with?"

"I was hoping you'd know. Pull over."

Englebretson turned down an alley, coming to a halt behind the base's darkened movie theater.

Bolan started to open the door, but the old man grabbed his arm. "Where are you going?"

"To find out what's going on."

"How? To find out what is in the crates, you would have to..." He let his voice trail off.

"Sneak on board the ship," Bolan said. "Ditch these wheels and go back to the van, Englebretson. If I'm not there in two hours, forget me."

Before Englebretson or his wife could object, the Executioner disappeared into the night.

6

Dozens of pages of continuous-feed computer paper covered Hal Brognola's desk in tangled masses. He dug under the mess, searching for the buzzing telephone. Scooping a coiled pile into each hand, he tried to stack them on the filing cabinet next to the desk.

The pages slipped from his grasp and accordioned back across the desk, covering the phone again as it continued to buzz.

The headache that had started slowly the night before now pounded incessantly, threatening to drive the big Fed's brain through his skull. He laid a forearm on the edge of the desk and in one swift, frustrated move, swept it across the surface. Pens, pencils and the twisted bundles of paper sailed to the floor. The phone went with it.

"Mr. Brognola? Mr. Brognola?" a tiny voice called from the disengaged receiver at Brognola's feet. "Mr.—"

Brognola retrieved the phone and pressed it to his ear. "What is it?" he growled.

"Mr. Lyons on four-four," his secretary said sheepishly.

"Thanks, Kelly," he said. "Sorry I jumped on you." He took a deep breath, and the pain shot through his brain again.

"No problem, sir. Should I put him through?"

Brognola rubbed his temple with his free hand. He had been without sleep for the past two nights, which had brought on a headache, and the headache had brought on irritability. "Yes," he said carefully. "Thank you." He waited a moment for the connection.

"Hal."

"Yeah, Ironman?"

Carl Lyons didn't waste any time. "I want us out of here, Hal. Now. There's better things we can be doing than—"

"You know I can't do that," Brognola interrupted. "You've got direct orders from the President."

"Look, Hal. This is crazy. Number one—if the Haakovians will just agree to adequate security measures, the Secret Service can handle this baby-sitting job as well as we can. And if they won't agree, nobody can do it. So if that's the case, there's no point wasting us—"

"I couldn't agree more. But you heard the Man. Just exactly what do you think I can—"

"You know what I want you to do. Get the President on the phone and get us out of here. He's a good President, Hal, and a good man. And I know he had *some* experience with the CIA. But he's hardly an expert in this arena. Convince him he's made a mistake."

Brognola's fingers moved to his temple again as the headache raged on. "I've already tried. Unless you've got some new ammunition to fire at him—"

"I do."

Brognola stopped. "Go on."

"We've had another hit attempt on the South. I ran the prints through the Farm. These weren't Stensvik's ex-KGB cronies and the like. This time, three gunners from the Medellín cartel tried to get in on the act."

Brognola stopped rubbing his head. "You're sure?"

"Fingerprints don't lie."

New pain shot through the G-man's skull. "Any chance these guys were free-lancing? Doing contract work for Medellín and hired out to Stensvik?"

Lyons sounded disgusted—not with Brognola, but with the whole situation. "Anything's possible, Hal. But the intel from the Farm sounded like they were full-time, union-card-holding dope dealers."

"Where are you now?" Brognola asked.

"Pay phone in the west wing, General Assembly building." Lyons read the number off the dial.

Brognola jotted it down on his desk pad. "I'll give the Man a call and get back with you, Ironman. Stay there. With any luck, we'll have you out of there and finding out where the cartel boys fit into the picture."

"Ten-four," Lyons said.

Brognola heard the line go dead.

The Justice man opened the bottom drawer of his desk, found the aspirin bottle and stuffed four tiny white pills into his mouth. The bitter taste hit him at the back of the jaws as he dialed the special-mission emergency number at the White House.

The President's personal secretary answered on the third ring.

"Hal Brognola," the Justice man said. "Is the President available?"

"Is this an emergency, Mr. Brognola?" the secretary asked suspiciously.

Brognola felt his temper rise. He forced his voice to remain calm. "I wouldn't tie up the emergency line if it wasn't."

"One moment."

Three minutes later, the Man picked up the line. "Yes, Hal?"

Brognola informed him about the new developments. The President listened quietly.

"Well, Hal," he said when the Justice man had finished, "I don't see how this changes anything. It would be a simple enough thing for Stensvik to hire some international thugs, wouldn't it?"

Brognola shook his head. The Man *was* a good President. But Lyons was right. Once in a while, he let the fact that he'd done a few years with the CIA convince him he was an expert at clandestine affairs. "Yes sir," the big Fed finally said, "but Lyons doesn't think so. Neither do I. We'd like permission to pull Able Team off of security and let them—"

"Hal, we've discussed this more than once. I'm walking a political tightrope between these two countries. Both leaders have requested that I place my very best operatives in charge of the protection of their representatives. That means Able Team.''

"Mr. President, I understand your position. But as you say, Carl Lyons is the best. For that reason I trust his judgment, and if he feels that this drug connection may be a key element—"

"It may very well be a key element, Hal," the Man said curtly. "So I suggest that you send agents to investigate. Any agents under your jurisdiction you feel are capable of performing the task." The President paused, then said, "Except Carl Lyons, Rosario Blancanales, and Hermann Schwarz. Do I make myself clear?"

"Yes, sir."

"Then good day." The line clicked dead in the Justice man's ear.

Brognola's head continued to throb as he got another dial tone and tapped the number Lyons had given him. The Able Team leader answered before the first ring had ended. "Yeah?"

"Sorry, Ironman," Brognola said. "It's no go."

There was a long pause at the end of the line. "That's what I figured," Lyons finally said. "Okay, there's other ways to make him change his mind."

"Carl, I don't know what you're planning, but—"

"Then hear me out, Hal. Normally I wouldn't go against the President, and you know it. But these are extraordinary conditions."

Brognola listened without interruption as the Able Team leader went on to outline a plan that would have turned most bureaucrats to jelly. When Lyons finished, the big Fed warned, "I hope you know what you're doing."

"Me, too. But there's no other choice, Hal. We've got to find out what's going on with the Colombians."

Brognola gripped his forehead as the hammers continued to pound. "I agree. Okay. Go ahead."

Lyons paused again, then said, "You know, Brognola, for a supervisor, you're not half-bad."

"You can kiss me later. Now get the hell off the phone and get this thing rolling."

"I will. But I wouldn't hold my breath for that kiss." He hung up.

Brognola dialed Stony Man Farm. He filled Price in on the conversation with Lyons.

"How about I get Leo Turrin on it?" Price suggested. "He can trace them back to their entry into the country. Probably farther." She hadn't seemed perplexed that Able Team was more or less "circling" the President.

"Good idea." He dropped the phone back into the cradle.

Turrin would be perfect. The ex-Mafia undercover man could use his vast network of Mob connections to check out the cartel gunmen's movements and lay the groundwork for Able Team.

Brognola swiveled in his chair and reached for his cigar box. What Lyons intended to do was crazy.

So crazy, it just might work.

"Oh, well," the Justice man said out loud as he opened the box. "If it works, maybe this damn headache will go away." He bit the tip off a long brown cigar and stuck the end in his mouth. "Of course if it doesn't work, I won't lose the headache," he muttered. "But I think I can be pretty damn sure of losing my job."

A GENTLY RISING HILL LED from the water to the perimeter fence surrounding Lenin naval base. A cracked concrete walkway paralleled the docks on one side, and separating the walk from the landscaped hill was a six-foot stem wall. Intermittent staircases led from the walk, through the wall and up the hill to several small entrance gates guarded by armed men. The staircases provided foot routes to and from the ships to the sailor bars that stood just outside the base.

Crouching slightly, Bolan crept silently through the shadows on the hill side of the wall, his senses acute to the seamen who passed on the other side. Although his combat blacksuit and weapons were hidden by the wool overcoat, it wouldn't do him any good to be spotted on base. Civilian attire meant he'd still be stopped for questioning, and that a curfew permit would be demanded.

The Executioner didn't have one. Particularly one that permitted him to be on a military base.

Bolan pulled the earflaps of the Russian *shrapki* over his ears, cloaking his features. If he was detected, his only chance would be to run for it, lose the easily remembered hat and coat, and attempt to get off base through the gate where Englebretson's men still posed as guards.

As he neared the freighter, the flag of Norway, its offset blue and white cross backed by red, appeared flapping atop the mast. Bolan saw the name *Monika Maria* on the hull near the bow. He continued to creep through the darkness. He paused to scan the area each time he reached one of the stairways, then skirted across the steps to the cover of the wall again.

Finally he stopped, leaning around a corner of the wall to survey *Monika Maria*. Dozens of dark, tiny figures scampered about the deck, gangplank and pier. Some of the figures carried the mysterious crates on and off the ship. Others, in uniform, stood quietly, their shadowy outlines holding Russian-made assault rifles.

Security was tight. Too tight for a simple cargo exchange.

And too tight to sneak aboard undetected.

Bolan crept on. As he drew even with the freighter, he saw a mixture of North Haakovian navy uniforms and the informal khaki and denim worn by Norwegian merchant mariners. Watches had been set out not only at the gangplank, but on the port and starboard sides of the ship, as well. And although he couldn't see the bow, the Executioner had no doubt that it would be guarded, too.

The warrior stopped behind the wall, a few feet from another staircase. On board the ship he saw a sailor drop the crate in his hands. The wooden box splintered, and dark square shapes scattered across the deck. Immediately several of the men stopped to gather them up again.

What had spilled from the crate? Bolan couldn't tell. He was still too far away.

The Executioner moved to the corner of the wall, peering through the darkness to the lights around the guard shack at the top of the hill. Beyond the shack, he could see the neon signs above the sailor bars. Leaving the wall, he inched up the hill, moving carefully, using whatever cover became available. He stopped halfway between the quayside and guard shack, taking concealment in a thicket of well-tended junipers.

Bolan closed his eyes, focusing on his ears. He half expected to hear the laughter and revelry of the drunken men loitering outside the taverns on the other side of the chain-link fence. Instead, only a dull murmur reverberated down the steps to meet his ears.

The Executioner knew the reason for the men's restraint without being told. North Haakovia was the final Communist stronghold in Europe. A place where the wrong words could get you life in a rat-infested gulag, perhaps even land you in front of a firing squad.

Even the drunks had learned it paid to keep quiet.

Bolan watched two weaving men in khakis approach the guard shack from the bars, seeking entrance to the base. They showed their passes, then staggered through the gate. The Executioner squinted through the darkness, eyeing both men, evaluating their height and weight.

One was well under six feet and couldn't have weighed more than one-fifty. The other stood about Bolan's height, but was as slender as his partner.

Neither man's uniform would fit the Executioner.

The duo mumbled incoherently as they walked carefully down the steps, passing two feet from where the Executioner hid, before descending on to the quayside.

The warrior let them pass.

Fifteen minutes later, a black sedan bearing the North Haakovian naval emblem pulled to a halt outside the gate. A man wearing an N.H. captain's uniform hurried out of the back seat, circled the car and opened the door on the other side.

A stunning woman with carefully coiffed red hair let him help her out, smoothed the folds of the formal gown that clung to her hips and took his arm. The captain leaned into the driver's window, said something to the driver and the car pulled away.

Bolan scrutinized the man as the couple turned toward the gate. A little over six feet and muscular. The uniform would fit.

The captain didn't bother to show ID or even salute as he led his date through the gate. Rank had its privileges, the warrior knew, and the captain's would allow Bolan to move about the ship with relative impunity. But the captain's clothes had a downside, as well. Too much rank. It would draw attention. And the captain's face would be well-known to the sailors.

And there was the woman.

Bolan continued to wait.

Twenty minutes later, a mixed party of North Haakovian naval men and Danish merchant mariners came staggering up to the gate. The Haakovians wore blue trench coats over their uniforms. The Danes had dressed in khaki pants, chambray shirts and faded denim overcoats. Passing a bottle of liquor back and forth, the group weaved unsteadily toward the guards at the gate.

One of the guards grabbed the bottle from a seaman. His voice rose through the night, evidently scolding the men for their condition. Finally he waved them through, and the party started down the steps.

As soon as they'd passed, the guard looked nervously around, then tipped the bottle to his lips before passing it to his partner.

Bolan sized the men up as they bounced wearily down the steps. Two of the men—a Haakovian lieutenant and a Danish sailor—were about the right size. But with so many men together, the only chance he'd have at one of their uniforms was if the lieutenant or sailor brought up the rear of the pack when they passed.

The Executioner crouched and waited.

The men's positions within the group changed as they neared, the tall Dane first leading the pack, then falling to the middle as another man produced a hidden bottle of vodka. The whole procession stopped while they each took a gulp, and when they moved out again, the Dane resumed the lead.

Thirty feet from where the Executioner lay in wait, the lieutenant increased his pace to get back to the bottle near the front. The Dane passed it to him, then dropped to the middle of the group.

Bolan frowned in exasperation as the big men leap-frogged back and forth, always at the front or middle of the group. Then, as they drew abreast of the Executioner, a short Haakovian grabbed for the vodka.

The bottle fell to the concrete and bounced down the steps without breaking, rolling under the lieutenant's foot as he took a step. The big lieutenant's feet flew up into the air as if he'd stepped on a banana peel.

Hoots and hollers of glee rose from the men as the Haakovian officer crashed drunkenly to the concrete. He rolled to his side, groaning, holding his ankle. The men continued to laugh, then the lieutenant rose to a sitting position, muttered something in Haakovian and waved toward the ships.

A Dane stooped to assist him, but the lieutenant brushed the man's hand off.

The Executioner let the rest of the men stumble down the steps, then moved cautiously through the bushes toward the edge of the steps. The lieutenant sat rubbing his ankle and cursing under his breath. Reaching out from the shrubs, Bolan circled an arm around the man's neck and cupped a hand over his mouth.

He felt the muffled scream against his fingers as he jerked the lieutenant into the bushes.

The Executioner rolled the man onto his back and drew a hand high over his head. His right fist drove down, crashing into the lieutenant's jaw with the sharp crack.

The naval officer's head could have been made out of iron. He moaned, but continued to struggle.

Bolan punched him again and he closed his eyes.

The Executioner moved quickly, undressing the lieutenant before doffing his coat and hat. The uniform fit snugly over the blacksuit, but it would work. He covered the Beretta and Desert Eagle with the lieutenant's trench coat, then rolled the unconscious man to his stomach and pulled two sets of plastic Flex-Cuffs from a pocket.

A moment later, the lieutenant's wrists and ankles were bound. A ripped sleeve from the Executioner's wool overcoat went into the Haakovian's mouth as a gag, and the naval officer was ready to sleep it off.

Without pausing, Bolan hurried down the steps after the party. The North Haakovians and Danes were still a good thirty yards from the docks when Bolan neared. He slowed, gradually making his way to the rear of the pack, his eyes scanning both the drunken men's backs and the docks ahead. By the time they reached the quayside, the Executioner was less than ten feet behind the Danish seaman who brought up the rear.

Bolan moved even closer, walking silently as they neared the Norwegian freighter. His eyes scanned ahead, watching other men in twos and threes mounting the gangway.

Good. The Danish seamen were showing ID, but the Haakovians were being passed through on uniform only.

The Executioner lowered his head slightly as the men ahead of him turned up the gangplank. He staggered slightly, moving to within a foot of the Danish seaman's back. He held his breath as he staggered past the North Haakovian watch and onto the deck of the *Monika Maria*.

The loading and unloading process was still in high gear as Bolan made his way across the deck. Men in khaki and denim carried wooden crates from the hold to the dock, while uniformed Haakovians bore similar cargo in the opposite direction. The Executioner fell in with a party of sailors, using the opportunity to peer down through the slats in the top of one of the crates.

A dark green metal box rested within the protective shell. Bolan caught a flash of yellow letters printed across the top of the metal.

The Executioner broke from the group as he neared the ladder leading down to the holds. He glanced quickly behind him and saw a naval guard gripping an AK-47 and frowning his way.

The warrior followed two sailors lugging one of the crates down the passageway toward the hold, knowing his luck was drawing to a close. He had seen the expression on the guard's face. It was an expression he had seen many times within the bureaucracy of the military.

Confusion. Indecision. The guard had spotted Bolan as an unfamiliar face. And unless he was a fool, the guard would know that could mean only one of two things: a new officer had been assigned to the ship or the lieutenant was an impostor.

Confusion. Indecision. Right now, the guard was experiencing the flip side of military order and obedience. He was struggling to decide whether to check papers and risk offending a newly stationed man of higher rank.

Bolan heard steps coming down the ladder behind him. Turning, he saw the shoes and pant legs of a N.H. navy uniform. The man's belt, and the hands gripping the AK-47, appeared next.

The Executioner didn't wait for a positive ID. He turned and shoved past the crate ahead of him. Behind him, a voice cried out in Haakovian.

The Executioner hurried down the corridor. Passing a connecting passageway, he saw more men toting crates lined up at the entryway to the hold. He turned, hearing the commotion as the deck guard shoved past the loaders behind him.

Without speaking, Bolan threaded his way through the men with the crates, letting the rank on his shoulders pave the way. When he entered the hold, he saw several more men stacking the crates at the rear of the storage area. To their left, a smaller entryway led down another passageway.

The Executioner marched to the crates. Squinting, he knelt as if to inspect a box against the wall. Behind him, the noise stopped as the men quit working to stare at his back and wonder just who he was.

Time had just about run out. There would be no opportunity to identify the cargo.

There might not even be time to get off the ship.

Bolan turned around and glanced up, giving the men his dirtiest get-back-to-work look. The racket began again as they resumed stacking the crates.

Bolan reached inside the trench coat, ripped two buttons from the uniform blouse and reached his blacksuit. His fingers traced quickly across the material until they found the correct zipper and pulled.

The long-range homing device fell into his hand.

The Executioner glanced quickly over his shoulder again. The men were hard at work.

Reaching down through the slats, Bolan slapped the magnetic side of the homer to a metal can and stood.

The deck guard shoved his way suddenly into the hold.

Bolan hurried toward the small side passageway. As he reached the opening, he heard the same voice he'd heard in the hall cry out again. This time, the bolt of the AK-47 slid home.

The Executioner turned to see the guard skirting around the stacked crates toward him.

The warrior walked quickly through the door, then broke into a sprint down the passageway. Spotting another ladder to the deck, he took the steps three at a time, then slowed and headed toward the gangplank.

As he passed the watch, the Executioner turned for one final glance across the deck. The loading and unloading was still in progress. Nothing out of the ordinary. Business as usual.

Bolan saluted the watch as he marched down the ramp and disappeared into the night.

7

Aaron Kurtzman's fingers flew across the keyboard. *Cayman Air Flight 1222: Dpt George Town 11:20 Arr Miami 12:47* flashed on the screen. The computer whiz tapped more buttons and the screen divided.

Three names, Frederico Alonzo Gonzales, Emmanuel Rosca Guttierez and Pedro Simon Lopez, appeared on the right-hand side of the monitor. On the other, the title Passenger Roster for Flight 1222 materialized.

Kurtzman began reading.

The computer wizard glanced down the ramp from his platform and saw Akira Tokaido call up one of the passenger lists for Southwest Airlines. The young Japanese man's samurai-style topknot bobbed over his head as he moved his denim-clad shoulders in time to whatever punk-rock CD now blasted from his player into the earplug. Beyond Tokaido sat Huntington Wethers and Carmen Delahunt. Wethers had taken the flights for TWA and sat frowning at his screen as he chewed the stem of his unlighted briar pipe. Carmen, looking her usual professional and petite self, typed away to call up another list from Delta.

All four of the Stony Man computer experts had stopped in midmission to search the passengers of all incoming flights from South America and the Caribbean.

Kurtzman turned back to his own screen. He touched the curser and moved slowly down the list. He held no illusions that any of them would find the names Gonzales, Guttierez, or Lopez on the screen. Drug-cartel hitmen didn't enter the U.S. under their own identities. But the computer ace knew that they had to start somewhere, and there was always the chance that the lists might hold some hidden clue.

Kurtzman continued to scan the names, pausing at Garcia. Just because the hitters from Colombia were Hispanic didn't mean they'd go with Hispanic names. They could have easily disguised themselves as Italians, Arabs, any dark-skinned ethnic group. And even if they had used Latino names, the three men in question would certainly not be the only Hispanics who'd entered the U.S. yesterday.

He continued to stare at the name Garcia. What was it that had caused him to stop? he asked himself. *Think.* He had to have seen something more than...

A tiny grin started at the corner of Kurtzman's mouth and spread as what had caught his eye finally registered in his conscious brain.

Frank Garcia. Frederico Gonzales. The names weren't only both Hispanic, they bore the same initials.

Coincidence? Probably.

Kurtzman pushed a key, flagged the name and went on.

The smile on Kurtzman's face grew. He glanced to the other side of the screen: Earl Gomez, Emmanuel Guttierez.

Another flag.

Kurtzman's grin faded slightly when he came to Lombardi. Italian. It didn't fit the pattern, but then again there was no hard evidence yet that there was a pattern—the whole thing could still just be coincidence. And even if he had stumbled onto a paradigm here, where was it written that the pattern couldn't be broken?

Pedro Lopez. Paul Lombardi. The initials were still the same. Kurtzman flagged the name and went on. He passed half a dozen more Hispanic names, two Italians and the Arabic surname Mudarrissi. But none of the initials matched those of the Colombia gunners, and when he came to Zuckerman, Kurtzman hit the Search button and returned to the flagged names.

Kurtzman felt a thrill rush through his body. He believed in his machines, believed in the near magic of which they were capable. But he believed even more in the oldest, most complex computer known to man—the human brain.

Even if what had now been entered into his brain was still no more than a hunch.

Kurtzman cleared the screen and exited the Cayman Air passenger list. He tapped into the airline's accounting department and called up the records for Flight 1222. When the new document appeared on the screen, he pressed the Search button, typed in *Garcia, Frank,* then pressed Search again.

The word Repositioning appeared in the bottom left-hand corner, then the curser stopped at Garcia. Kurtzman scanned past the flight specs and came to the payment record for the one-way ticket near the end of Garcia's file—$255.86 Chase Manhattan Visa. The Visa-card number and expiration date appeared last. The Stony Man computer wizard grabbed a pencil from the holder next to his monitor and jotted it down.

Kurtzman hit Search again and found the file for Earl Gomez. The price was the same, and payment had been made by the same credit card. The grin returned to his face as he sent the curser searching for Paul Lombardi. A short snicker escaped his lips when the Chase Manhattan number showed up again.

He felt the excitement shoot through his veins as he cleared the screen, exited the Cayman Air linkup and tapped into the records of Chase Manhattan bank. Working his way swiftly around several coded traps, he drew up the list of accounts for Chase's Visa customers and typed in the credit-card number. The account number and a company name appeared almost immediately, and Kurtzman couldn't restrain a laugh. He saw Tokaido's head swivel up to stare at him. The other computer techs followed suit. Kurtzman swung his wheelchair to face them and said, "Call off the hunt and get back to your other jobs, guys. I've got the lead we wanted."

The phone next to him rang shrilly, and Kurtzman turned to pick it up.

"Striker on 44," Barbara Price said.

Kurtzman pressed the button and heard Bolan's voice come over the line from the Baltics. "Got a job for you, Bear," Bolan said, and quickly ran down the story of the Norwegian ship and the homing device he had planted.

"I'll get right on it, big guy," Kurtzman replied. As quickly as Bolan's voice had appeared in his ear, it was gone.

Kurtzman got a dial tone, then hit the intercom button. Price picked it up.

"Yes, Aaron?"

"Turrin packed and ready?"

"He just called in. He's waiting to see where to start."

"Miami." He gave Price the info he'd gathered on the Colombian hit men's point of entry.

There was a long pause on Price's end of the line. "Okay," the Stony Man mission controller finally said. "I understand that the initials match up, they're all pseudonyms that a dark-skinned man could get away with, and all three tickets were purchased by the Martinez Construction Company. But what makes you so sure these aren't just three employees here on construction business? Martinez could hire an Italian, you know."

Kurtzman chuckled. "Yes, that's right. That's always possible. But we didn't find anything better, and there's one thing that leads me to believe there are just too many coincidences in this little scenario, Barb."

"Yeah?"

"Yeah. Martinez Construction's home office is in Medellín, Colombia."

"I'll get Leon on the move," she said. "And I'm sending two planes to follow the Norwegian ship. We'll back up your beeper with some visual surveillance."

"Good idea." Kurtzman replaced the receiver and twirled his wheelchair around, using the overdeveloped muscles in his forearms to propel himself across the platform to another set of computer banks. Pressing the On button on the side of one massive monitor, he waited for the machine to warm up.

Tokaido stood up at his terminal below, stretched his arms over his head, yawned, then performed three lightning-fast *chu,* or "head," blocks. "Ah," he said. "Circulation, at last. Bear, I'm going for some decaf. Want to come?"

Kurtzman shook his head as he began programming the computer. "No time," he called down the ramp. "I've got a boat to find."

THE SECRET SERVICE agents, combined with the reinforcement of Stony Man troops, outnumbered the delegations from North and South Haakovia six to one as they marched down the hall. Gadgets Schwarz got a sudden flash of déjà vu as the two groups left the General Assembly building and stopped on the curb in front of a long line of waiting limousines.

The Able Team electronics specialist suddenly remembered a time when he'd been a child, and his father had taken him to the zoo. The zookeepers had been getting ready to clean the tiger's pen, and were transferring the animal to temporary quarters in a small cage on wheels. The tiger rode quietly along the stone path, past a cage of frightened wildebeests. He barely gave other animals a second glance.

But the ten-year-old Schwarz had gotten the definite impression that the tiger was watching the wildebeests carefully, waiting for any chance that presented itself to turn the animals into dinner.

He got that same impression now as he watched the nonchalance the North Haakovian representatives appeared to be exhibiting toward their counterparts from the South.

Carl Lyons, his Colt Python hanging at arm's length from his right hand, appeared at Schwarz's side. "You and Pol get the Northerners into their rooms fast." He stared ahead at the street, watching the Uzi-armed Secret Service agents who stood around the limos. "Post four of our troops and an agent in each room. Keep up a roving patrol of the halls. I don't want any of these guys leaving their rooms for any reason."

Schwarz nodded. "They know what's happening yet?"

Lyons snorted. "Some of it. They know I've declared this an emergency situation. They know they're switching hotels whether they like it or not, and that both sides will be in temporary protective custody."

"They aren't squawking too loud, so I get the feeling they don't understand what 'temporary' means. At least *your* definition, Ironman. You did put a little extra emphasis on it, so should I consider that the operative word?"

Lyons continued to stare at the street. His poker face didn't change. "You should."

Schwarz grinned as what Lyons had planned suddenly sank in. He and Blancanales teased the ex-cop almost unmercifully about being tight and rigid, even insinuating sometimes that he had no imagination and worked like a machine. But when it came right down to it, Carl Lyons was a pretty damn creative guy.

"They'll be on the phone bitching to Stensvik and Varkaus in no time," Schwarz said.

It looked like a trace of a smile pulled at Lyons's lips, but Schwarz couldn't be sure. The Able Team leader turned to face him. "I'm counting on it." The big ex-LAPD detective got in next to the driver of the lead South Haakovian limousine.

Schwarz opened the door and got into the last car. In the first seat behind him, Olaf Kristiansson and Gustaf Terskol sat shoulder to shoulder with two Secret Service men. In the rear, Vladimir Bergman was squeezed between two Stony Man soldiers dressed in gray pin-striped suits and the most outlandish ties Schwarz had ever seen. He turned back to the General Assembly building as Blancanales exited in the midst of another group of bodyguards and diplomats, and got into the limo in front of him.

The procession pulled away from the curb and started up First Avenue toward the Queensboro Bridge. The men in the rear seats remained silent as the driver turned left, away from the river, and started along 59th Street. Then Terskol cleared his throat, and said, "You have not told us where we are going."

Schwarz turned and rested an arm over the seat. "Plaza Hotel. One of the best in the world. You'll love it."

Terskol nodded. "You have stayed there?"

Schwarz laughed. "On what they pay *me?* You must be kidding. No, never stayed there, but I've heard about it. Trust me. It's supposed to be great."

Terskol's gray eyebrows furrowed in concern. "How long will we be there?"

Schwarz shrugged and turned back to the windshield. "I don't know. But it's just temporary, they tell me." He paused, then glanced back over his shoulder. "It's all for your own good, you understand."

He got no answer.

Ahead to their right Schwarz saw Central Park South, and then suddenly they were pulling into the Plaza's parking garage. Lyons got out of the lead vehicle and walked back along the convoy, stopping briefly to lean down and say something to each driver as he passed.

When he reached Schwarz's vehicle, the driver tapped the button, lowering the window.

"We'll be exiting the cars in an orderly fashion," Lyons instructed. "Your car will be last. Leave your luggage, and it will be brought to your rooms as soon as you're settled." Before the men in back could say anything, he spun on his heel and walked away.

"This will take forever," Olaf Kirstiansson said with a sigh.

Schwarz shrugged. "Better safe than sorry."

With excruciating slowness, the operation began. Lyons opened the door of the first limo and Karl Mentznof of the Southern delegation stepped out. He was immediately surrounded by two dozen agents. The party walked across the parking garage and disappeared into the building.

The men in the back seat sat quietly. Five minutes later, several of the agents returned to the garage.

Lyons opened the door again, and another man stepped out.

Vladimir Bergman blew air between his clenched teeth in exasperation. "Why must we enter one at a time?" he demanded. "It will take all afternoon!"

Schwarz turned and looked over the seat. "Security precaution," he said simply. "It's for your own good."

After another five minutes, the agents reappeared and another delegate got out and entered the building with them.

"Good God!" Terskol fumed. "What takes them so long?"

"Oh, you know," Schwarz said. "Got to check in, do all that paperwork and everything."

"Why wasn't that taken care of ahead of time?" Terskol demanded.

"Sorry. We were too busy trying to keep you folks from getting shot."

By the time Lyons and the guards reached Schwarz's limo nearly an hour later, the North Haakovian representatives were ready to pull their hair out. The Able Team leader opened the door to the back seat and pointed to Terskol. The man shot out of the car and headed toward the hotel in the midst of the guards.

Schwarz joined the last group of guards escorting Kristiansson into the building. They stopped at the main desk in the lobby and waited while the North Haakovian filled out a registration card. "This is an insult," he hissed as he scribbled his name at the bottom of the card. "President Stensvik will be informed."

Schwarz shrugged. "Like I said before, it's all for your own good." He took the key from the desk clerk and smiled. "Allow me," he said, and led the procession to the ornately decorated antique elevator doors. He watched Kristiansson fiddle nervously with the grip of his briefcase as the car rose to the fourth floor. When the doors opened again, Schwarz escorted the procession down the hall to room 422, opened the door and stepped back.

Schwarz followed Kristiansson into the huge forty-by-forty-foot room and almost gasped when he saw the decor. He'd been right, the place *was* the best. The room was richly appointed with dark oak Victorian furniture, and prints of Van Goghs and Monets were positioned here and there on the walls.

Pushing past Kristiansson, Schwarz hurried to the bathroom and opened the door. It was almost half as large as the bedroom, and the word *palatial* came to mind.

All in all, it was the most beautiful prison Gadgets Schwarz had ever seen.

He turned back to Kristiansson. "Well, sir," he said. "I'll have to be going now. But these gentlemen will stay here to keep you company." He indicated the four gray-clad Stony Man troops and a Secret Service agent.

Kristiansson flopped to his back on the bed and crossed his arms over his chest. "I do not desire any companionship, thank you."

"They'll be staying just the same."

The North Haakovian rose to a sitting position. "What?"

"Security, sir. Like I said before, it's for—"

"My own good," Kristiansson finished for him. "Yes, I know." He swung his legs over the side of the bed. "How long is this going to last?"

Schwarz shrugged. "It's temporary."

Kristiansson shook his head disgustedly and stood. "I am hungry," he said. "Show me to the dining room."

"Sorry again, sir. Nobody leaves his room. Why don't you call room service? I hear the Palm Court downstairs has got a brunch you wouldn't believe. Or maybe you'd rather have a pizza. Or we could send out for some Chinese. Or—"

"You are a son of a bitch!" the North Haakovian suddenly roared at the top of his lungs. "I am going to call President Stensvik right now!" He strode to the telephone, then stopped and whirled to face Schwarz. "But I suppose the phone has been disconnected for security reasons, too," he said sarcastically. "Temporarily, of course. And for my own good."

Schwarz couldn't fight back the smile. "Oh, no sir," he said. "Go right ahead. The phone should be working just fine. And if it isn't, we'll find you one that is. That's a promise."

ONE FORTY-EIGHT ROLFE stood on the corner of a residential section near Helsinki's South Harbor. The stars of night had given way to the early-morning sun as Gary Manning, behind the wheel of the station wagon, passed the house.

One-story, frame. Similar to the one they'd just come from. No lights on. Had all of Vaino's men gone to sleep?

Not likely.

Manning drove another block and a half before pulling over to the curb. He got out, opened the rear door and pulled the terrorist out. Yanking off the man's blindfold, he pointed to the house. "That it?"

"Yes. That is the house."

Katz stepped forward. He wore the pin-striped coveralls again, and the toolbox dangled once more from his prosthetic arm. "You will be coming with us," he said to the terrorist. "And if anything goes wrong, you will be the first to die." He drew a forefinger across the man's throat, indicating the method of his demise.

Turning toward the rest of the group, Katz said, "Same plan, similar assignments. Rafael, come with me to the front door. Calvin, take the rear; David, the east-side windows. I saw only one window on the west side as we passed. Gary, cover it. Take our friend here with you."

The party took off down the street, walking silently, close to the darkened houses and away from the streetlights. James separated himself again as they neared the corner, cutting down the alley toward the back.

Manning shoved his hostage ahead of him and took off for the west side while McCarter stopped when they drew abreast of it. As he pushed the terrorist around the corner, Manning saw Katz and Encizo start up the steps to the porch.

He rounded the corner, turned back and faced the window.

The next thing Gary Manning knew, a rifle barrel broke through the glass and a volley of automatic fire streaked toward him.

His hostage went down under the fire as Manning hit the ground. In the corner of his eye, the big Canadian saw a burst of crimson erupt from the terrorist's throat and chest. The man rolled to his back, his arms and legs jerking spasmodically. Then he stopped moving.

Manning dropped the front sight of his Uzi on the window and returned fire, a volley of 9 mm rounds exploding from the subgun and peppering the window and the trim around it.

The rifle barrel jumped back into the house.

The Phoenix Force warrior didn't let up. Keeping the trigger back against the guard, he timed the burst mentally, using enough ammo to cover his next move without letting the rifle run dry. When he estimated the magazine to still hold three to five rounds, he let up on the trigger, vaulted to his feet and sprinted toward the house.

Another burst erupted from the window and flew past as Manning tapped a round through the opening. The volley continued, and the big Canadian let loose with two more rounds.

The assault ended as the bolt of his Uzi blew back for the last time.

Manning hit the ground on his shoulder, rolling to cover beneath the window as his right hand jerked the Colt Gold Cup .45 from the holster on his hip. Holding the Uzi under his armpit, he fished another mag out of the carrier on his belt and slammed it into the weapon with his left.

Before he could chamber a round, another rifleman shot through the window. As the man's weapon tilted toward Manning, he dived to the side, and a burst of autofire blasted into the grass where he'd lain a moment before.

To the side of the window now, Manning rose to his knees. He stuck the Gold Cup through the window and felt soft flesh give as the muzzle struck someone in the belly. He pulled the trigger, then jerked his arm back outside. Blood covered his hand.

For the first time the Canadian heard gunfire from the other parts of the house. Phoenix Force had met a well-readied defense, which meant Vaino and his men had been tipped off to their approach. Maybe they'd seen the van drive by. Maybe they'd seen the men walking down the street carrying the trash bags, or maybe someone back at the other house had escaped and alerted them.

Manning knew they'd probably never know where the leak came from. But it hardly mattered. Right now, the important thing was staying alive and finding Vaino.

The big Canadian chambered a round into the Uzi and shoved the Gold Cup back in its holster. He fired a 3-round burst through the window, dropped below the sill and crawled to the other side. Firing another burst at the new angle, he took a deep breath, then dived through the opening.

Sharp slivers of glass remained around the edges of the window. They sliced through Manning's shoulders and side like razors as he sailed into the room and fell to the floor. Landing on his side, he rolled to his belly, the Uzi up and tracking.

Except for the bodies of the two men he'd shot from the outside, the bedroom was empty. Manning glanced around. Spartan provisions: bare walls, little furniture, just half a dozen bare mattresses arranged side by side on the floor.

Another safehouse, all right.

Automatic fire continued from the rest of the house, and Manning jumped to his feet. He moved cautiously to the door. Peering into the hall, he saw a man wearing a rough sheepskin vest. Facing away, the man knelt to the side of an archway that led to the living room. He fired a Belgian FN Herstal machine pistol around the corner, but jumped back, hugging the wall as an unseen gun answered his assault.

Manning recognized the distinctive sound of the weapon in the living room—Katz's Steyr.

Stepping out of the bedroom, the big Canadian point-shot, sending a dozen 9 mm rounds down the hall to stitch up the terrorist's back. Holes appeared in the sheepskin vest, then disappeared beneath the blood as the wool lining danced through the air like falling snow flakes.

Manning stepped over the body, his Uzi at the ready. Gunfire still sounded from the rear of the house, but unless his ears were deceiving him, it had slowed. That meant someone was winning the battle.

Footsteps ran toward him. Manning took a step back from the archway, his hands tensing on the subgun. A short burst of fire sounded from Katz's Steyr, then a blurry form dressed in blue jeans and a gray leather jacket spun recklessly through the archway and into the hall.

Abruptly the house fell quiet.

A moment later, the big Canadian heard Katz's voice. "Sound off!" the Phoenix Force leader ordered.

The Cuban's voice came from the living room. "Encizo!"

From the rear of the house, Manning heard a distant, "James!" and then a heavy British accent said, "McCarter," from the same general area.

"Manning!" the Canadian cried and started toward the living room.

"Advance with caution!" Katz ordered.

Manning started to pass what looked to be a utility closet, then stopped. Slinging his subgun, he drew the Gold Cup. Then, standing to the side of the door, he twisted the knob and threw it back.

A Skorpion machine pistol and two hands appeared in the opening. In the darkened closet the hands and gun looked almost unattached, as if they were floating in the air, free of a body.

Manning squeezed the trigger and sent a double-tap of 230-grain .45s into the darkness where he knew the rest of the man had to be.

The Skorpion clattered to the floor, then the hands turned palms up, as if pleading for life. But the eyes of the terrorist were already closed as he fell forward into the hall.

Manning hurried into the living room.

Katz spoke up quickly. "Okay," he said. "We don't have much time. Half the shooting took place outside the house, which means the neighbors heard it and the police will already be on their way." He cleared his throat. "I'm afraid I already know the answer to this, but did anybody get Vaino?"

Four negative responses.

"Anybody see him?"

Katz got a chorus of nos.

"Our prisoner?" he asked.

"Went down in the first wave," Manning replied.

"Okay," the Israeli went on. "As I said, there isn't much time. Search this place. We've got to find something that will lead us to Vaino, or at the least to another one of his hideouts."

James held up a hand. "Think I've already found it." He nodded over his shoulder, then turned and led the party out of the living room, down another hall, toward the back door where he'd entered. Turning into what Manning figured was a rear bedroom, he motioned for the rest of the team to follow.

Manning brought up the rear, stepping into the room to see that he'd been only partially correct. The room might have been built to serve as a bedroom.

But it had been converted into a war room.

Charts and photographs of various sites around Helsinki and other European cities covered the walls. The only furniture was a long conference table along one wall and the eight metal folding chairs that surrounded it.

Manning moved quickly to the conference table. Blueprints and maps covered the surface. He leaned forward, resting both arms on the edge as he scanned the collection. The big Canadian's eyes fell on a map of the city. Something had been circled in red ink.

He picked up the map. The Helsinki city hall.

Handing the map to Katz, Manning said, "Anything scheduled at city hall in the near future that might be of interest to Vaino?"

"A speech."

"Who's giving it?"

"Risto Kalle."

"When?"

Katz looked down at his watch, then back up at Manning. "It started ten minutes ago."

Without another word Katzenelenbogen turned and headed for the door.

Manning, and the rest of Phoenix Force, followed.

8

Dawn had broken by the time the Executioner saw the North Haakovian army truck appear on the road leading to the base. He watched from behind a row of trees as the vehicle passed. As soon as it was gone, he emerged, sprinted across the road and entered the forest.

Following the orders he'd given Goran Englebretson, Hans and Erik had abandoned the guard shack by the time he'd made it back to the gate thirty minutes earlier. But the bodies of the guards who'd tried to rape Ingmarie hadn't yet been discovered, and the Executioner had walked boldly through the gate, still wearing the lieutenant's uniform.

But as he hurried toward the spot where they'd hidden the van the night before, the Executioner wondered if the freedom fighters had followed all of his orders and left the area when he didn't return within the time he'd allowed.

They hadn't. Hans sat behind the wheel of the van, Englebretson in the front seat next to him. Erik and Ingmarie were in the back. "You are late." Englebretson grinned. "In Haakovia, that is considered very rude."

"You have my apologies," he said as Erik slid the side door open and he vaulted into the back.

Englebretson turned around to face him as Hans started the engine. "So," he said. "What are they loading onto the ship?"

Bolan shook his head as Hans pulled the creaking Chevy onto the road and made a U-turn back toward Sturegorsk. "I didn't have time to find out. But I've marked them. My people will be following the ship's every move." He jerked slightly as Hans floored the accelerator. Slowly the ancient Chevy picked up speed.

"How about the off-coming load? Know anything?" the Executioner asked.

Englebretson shook his head. "Not yet. But we watched them transfer the crates to a truck." He pointed ahead, through the windshield. "The truck that just went by. You must have seen it."

"I did." Bolan glanced around at the van. "Can this thing catch it?"

The old man smiled. "Eventually. If they don't get where they're going before we can find them."

Hans practically stood up in his seat, putting all of his weight on the accelerator and appearing to try to mentally transfer his enthusiasm to the Chevy's engine. It took nearly a minute to reach sixty miles per hour, but as they did, they rounded a curve and the transport vehicle appeared ahead on the road.

"Slow down," Englebretson ordered, glancing at his watch. "Curfew is in effect for seven more minutes."

Hans lifted his foot and the van slowed to fifty.

Bolan settled in, taking advantage of the situation to close his eyes for a few minutes. But sleep wouldn't come, so he opened them again, watching the truck ahead and considering the angles.

They needed to know what was leaving North Haakovia on the Norwegian freighter, but they also needed to find out what the ship had brought into the country. If it was important enough to warrant the vast amount of security he'd seen on the *Monika Marie,* it was important enough to investigate. And there were only two ways that could be done: hijack the vehicle while it was on the road, or continue to follow it to its destination before striking. Both options had negative aspects.

If they hit the truck on the road, there was always the chance they'd be spotted. But if they waited, the truck might very well lead them onto another military base where pursuit would have to be cut off.

Considering the problems, the answer became easy.

A few minutes later, Englebretson announced, "Curfew . . . off," he said.

Bolan leaned toward the old man. "Ingmarie was a terrific decoy last night. You mind using her again?"

"It is never something I enjoy, but if it is necessary, we will do it."

Ingmarie shifted in her seat next to Bolan. "You might ask *me* what *I* mind."

"Sorry. That was my next question."

The offended look vanished from the woman's face. She smiled up at the Executioner, her eyes sparkling like emeralds under a jeweler's glass. "I am here to help the cause, just like the men. What do you have in mind?"

Bolan told her. Ingmarie's eyebrows furrowed momentarily, then she nodded. "It should work."

Englebretson stood and moved through the space between the seats to the back of the van. Ingmarie took his place and reached over to grasp the steering wheel.

Hans pulled himself carefully away from the wheel and squeezed into the back as Ingemarie slid into the driver's seat.

Bolan and the other men crouched on the floor, out of sight.

Ingmarie stepped on the accelerator and the van chugged forward. A mile later, they drew even with the slow-moving transport truck. Bolan saw Ingmarie flash a smile through the window as they pulled ahead.

"They show interest, my sweet?" Englebretson asked from the back.

"Of course, dear." Ingmarie giggled. "They are men."

By the time the outskirts of Sturegorsk appeared in the distance, they were a mile ahead of the army truck. Ingmarie pulled the van around a curve and onto the shoulder. Killing the engine, she jumped out. Through the windshield, the Executioner saw her raise the hood, then look toward the road.

Bolan heard the truck approach and pulled the sound-suppressed Beretta from under his trench coat.

The air brakes hissed as the transport truck slowed then pulled to a halt just ahead of them. A young man of twenty or so jumped down from the cab. His face was pitted with acne, and his blond hair looked as if it hadn't been washed since puberty. He rested his hand on the holstered pistol at his side as he strutted importantly back to the van.

Ingmarie smiled and said something.

The soldier shook his head, then reached for her breast.

Ingmarie removed his hand and continued the conversation.

The soldier shook his head once more, then shrugged and turned back toward his vehicle.

Ingmarie said something, and he turned to her, a wicked leer on his face. She headed toward the side door of the van, her face a mask of resignation.

Bolan gritted his teeth as the soldier followed her to the door. Although he hadn't heard their words, and wouldn't have understood them if he had, the Executioner knew he'd just witnessed the Haakovian version of the old "Put out or walk" routine. Ingmarie either performed sexual favors for the young soldier, or he'd leave her on the road to rot.

The door slid open and the woman hurried in. A second later, the soldier appeared at the opening.

The smirk evaporated when he saw Bolan.

The Executioner reached out, grasped the young man by the throat and jerked him into the van. Englebretson slid the door closed.

Rolling the soldier to his back on the floor, Bolan brought the Beretta down hard across the man's jaw. The soldier closed his eyes and fell limp. Erik reached forward, unsnapped the flap on the would-be rapist's holster and relieved him of his weapon.

Bolan shoved him toward Erik and Hans and handed them two sets of Flex-Cuffs. They bound the man hand and foot, then sat back.

Bolan and the freedom fighters waited.

Ten minutes went by. Then fifteen. Finally the driver's door of the truck opened and an older soldier got out of the vehicle and started back toward the van. When he reached the door, he knocked. Getting no response, he pounded harder and yelled something in Haakovian.

Hans leaned in close to the Executioner. "He wants his turn."

"Let's give it to him," Bolan said. Ripping the door open, he grabbed a handful of the man's shirtfront and pulled him into the van.

The soldier twisted as he came flying through the door, his hand falling to the Lahti 9 mm pistol on his hip. He had it halfway out of the flap holster when the Beretta spit two rounds into his chest.

Bolan shook the young soldier back to consciousness. Blinking wetly, the North Haakovian tried to focus his eyes. The Executioner pressed the Beretta's suppressor under his nose. "Somebody ask him how many more men are in the truck."

Englebretson did the honors. The frightened young man shook his head when he answered.

Erik translated. "He says there were only the two of them."

Bolan cocked the Beretta for effect. "Tell him I don't believe it. They aren't going to send half the North Haakovian army and navy to guard the ship and then entrust whatever it brought to two men with pistols."

Englebretson translated. The soldier shook his head again.

"Keep him covered," Bolan said. "I'll go find out." He flipped the Beretta to safety and stuck it in his belt behind his back. Glancing quickly through the window, he checked up and down the road for traffic. Clear.

Bolan straightened his lieutenant's uniform, jumped out of the van and walked to the cab of the truck.

Empty. Just like the soldier had said.

Retracing his steps to the rear of the vehicle, he stopped in front of the canvas flap covering the cargo area. The faint metallic sound of a rifle bolt closing caught his ear.

The Executioner drew the Beretta and thumbed the selector to 3-round mode in one swift, fluid movement. He fired blindly through the flap, emptying the clip with five quick bursts.

To his rear he heard another vehicle chugging down the road. Drawing the Desert Eagle, he tore the shredded canvas to the side and dived inside, out of sight.

He found himself on top of twenty wooden crates and three more dead North Haakovian soldiers, assault rifles still gripped in their dead fingers.

Bolan pulled the tattered canvas flap back into place a second before the oncoming vehicle passed. He watched through a hole as the black ZIL slowed. The man behind the wheel looked curiously at the truck, then shrugged and drove on.

The Executioner rolled one of the bodies to the side and pulled the Cold Steel Magnum Tanto from his belt. Using the nine-inch blade as a pry bar, he flipped open the nearest lid.

Air escaped his lips in a rush when he saw what the crates contained.

Carefully stacked on top of one another were clear plastic freezer bags. Bolan lifted one from the top, hefting it in his hand to estimate the weight.

It would be 2.2 pounds. One kilo. He knew. It was hardly the first time the Executioner had seen cocaine.

North Haakovia. Home of the world's toughest drug laws. One of Stensvik's aces in the hole for landing a UN seat.

Well, Stensvik's operation had been unconventional and mysterious from the beginning, and Mack Bolan still didn't have all the answers.

But things were beginning to fall into place.

KURTZMAN PRESSED the phone harder into his ear. Anger flooded his veins, and for perhaps the hundredth time since he'd been robbed of the use of his legs, he wished he could kick some ass personally instead of just arranging for it to be done electronically.

There'd be so much more personal satisfaction in feeling the flesh against his shoe.

"Sammy," Kurtzman told the man on the other end, "I hate to be rude, but to tell you the truth I don't give a rat's ass about your 'technical difficulties.' I've got a boat to locate, I need that satellite hookup to get it done, and if this screen doesn't light up and start beeping in the next five minutes I'm coming down there personally and wrap this wheelchair around your ears. Clear?"

The Stony Man technician cleared his throat on the other end of the line. "It's clear, Bear."

"Then get the hell off the line and get me a picture."

Kurtzman heard a click in his ear. He settled back in the wheelchair and stared at the darkened monitor screen. A momentary flush of guilt replaced the anger. Sammy was doing his best—and he *was* the best at what he did. If he wasn't, he wouldn't be at Stony Man Farm. Sometimes "technical difficulties" really did come up, problems that were beyond even the scope of the best. And they took awhile to iron out.

Moments later the screen lighted up with a map of the Baltic Sea and the eastern half of the Atlantic Ocean.

A tiny light flashed on the western coast of the Iberian peninsula—Bolan's Norwegian ship.

Kurtzman felt his heart jump.

Something was wrong. Damn wrong.

He picked up the phone and hit Price's number on the intercom. Then, as was his custom, he turned to watch her through the glass dividing wall that separated him from the mission control room.

"Barb," he said as soon as she'd answered, "tell me I'm not going crazy."

"No more than usual."

"Striker did say he'd hooked the bug to a Norwegian cargo freighter, right?"

"That's what he said."

"And he was in North Haakovia. In the north part of the Baltic when he did it?"

"Affirmative again."

Kurtzman sucked in a breath. "Then can you tell me how this freighter got all the way down to port in Lisbon since then?"

The line was silent. Then Price said, "No, I can't." After another pause, she said, "But I can tell you this. I sent two pilots to locate the thing from the air. They were supposed to notify me as soon as they had it in sight. That should have happened by now, but I haven't heard anything."

"I'll get back to you," Kurtzman said. A moment later, he had Sammy on the line again. "Something's wrong."

"Look, Bear, the hookup is working. You're tapped into a NASA floater and it's perfect. Whatever the problem is, it isn't on this end."

Kurtzman hung up again. He leaned back against his chair and pressed his fingers together under his chin. A short somewhere in his computer bank? Interference from another hookup?

Where was the problem? Cargo ships simply didn't move with the speed of nuclear—

Kurtzman scooped the phone up again and jabbed Price's number. "Where did Striker attach the homing device?"

"To one of the crates," Price said. "You didn't know that?"

"It never occurred to me to ask."

"You think whatever's in them might be distorting the signal?"

Kurtzman paused, considering the possibility. "No," he finally said. "What I'm thinking is far more simple than that. Besides, the homer is insulated and monodirected. Even nearby electronic pulses shouldn't have any effect." He stopped to catch his breath as the excitement rose in his chest. "They've transferred the crate to another vessel, that's all."

"Hold on a minute."

Kurtzman heard a click in his ear as he went on hold.

Price was back in moments. "That was one of the surveillance planes," she said. "They finally spotted the freighter. It's anchored in Copenhagen."

"That makes more sense."

"Aaron, you want me to send them to Lisbon?"

"No. Just because they transferred the crate with the homer doesn't mean they've transferred *all* the cargo. Tell them to keep the ship in sight." The flash on the screen suddenly sounded three fast staccato beeps. Kurtzman looked up at the monitor to see the word Moving appear in the lower right-hand corner. The flashing light started across the Atlantic toward America. "Besides, if they've got the crate in what I think they do, the planes would never spot it anyway."

Suddenly the light went off and the beep ended.

Kurtzman didn't panic. By now, he'd figured out the problem, and he'd expected the vessel to disappear. He tapped a few more keys, then typed *underwater acoustic tracking* and hit the Enter button.

The beep and light reappeared a short distance west of where he'd lost them.

There was only one craft he knew of capable of making the trip from the Northern Baltic to Lisbon in the length of time this one had. A Russian SSN nuclear submarine of the Mike class. Constructured of titanium, the Mikes had their own liquid-cooled reactors.

Kurtzman hit more keys, dividing the screen, and a map of the rest of the Atlantic, the Caribbean and the Gulf of Mexico appeared on the right-hand side of the monitor. Flagging Lisbon, he entered the present location of the sub, then sat back as the computer clicked away, predicting the destination.

Fifteen seconds later, the words Present Course: Northern Caribbean appeared on the screen.

Kurtzman frowned. That could mean anything from Florida to Puerto Rico.

With Cuba sitting in the bull's-eye of the computer's predicted course.

"Okay," Kurtzman said out loud, "that makes sense. Stensvik and Castro—one commie to another. The last of the dying breed."

Just then the intercom buzzed again. Kurtzman lifted the receiver.

"Striker just hung up again," Price said. "The ship brought millions of dollars of cocaine to North Haakovia."

Kurtzman felt his gut tie up suddenly.

What was Stensvik using to pay for the coke? It had to be whatever was on the freighter and sub.

He looked back to the beep on the screen.

And when was the last time they grew that much dope in Cuba?

No, this wasn't just a simple exchange of products between Cuba and North Haakovia. There had to be more angles to this deal. And it was like opening up a can of worms. Each time they learned one bit of information, it opened the door to a dozen new mysteries.

Kurtzman returned the screen to the tracker and watched the sub head toward Cuba. Then, rolling back to the other computer, he wiped the sweat off his forehead and started typing.

Somebody had to put all these things together and come up with something that made sense. Well, Striker had his way of doing things, Able Team and Phoenix Force, theirs.

And Aaron Kurtzman had his, the computer man thought. As his fingers raced across the keyboard, a funny thought occurred to him.

He didn't type with the speed of a bullet, maybe.

But sometimes his computer keys could be just as lethal.

HAL BROGNOLA FIGURED it would take at least two hours.

It took less than thirty minutes.

"Please hold for the President," the voice on the other end of the line said.

The big Fed waited, the muscles in his neck tightening. The headache was still with him. The dull throb at the base of his skull that had started the night before, gotten worse when he'd talked to the President, and worse yet when he learned what Carl Lyons had planned, now enveloped him from scalp to neck and threatened to explode.

Three minutes later, the Man came on the line. "Hal?"

Brognola took a deep breath. "Yes, sir?"

The President's voice sounded tired, overworked. But through the obvious fatigue, Brognola detected the controlled anger. "I'm not sure exactly what Able Team thinks they're pulling, but in the past fifteen minutes I've had President Varkaus and President

Stensvik on the line. They're screaming that their people are prisoners."

"No, sir," he said, his voice even, confident. "After all that's happened, I felt it mandatory that the diplomats from both sides be given protective custody. At least for a few days until things quiet down."

The President cleared his throat. "Hal, Stensvik and Varkaus are both demanding that their people be released to lobby again."

"Sir, I don't believe that to be a very wise—"

"Stensvik and Varkaus are also demanding that whatever clowns I've placed in charge of security be removed and replaced with more respectful personnel. I told them I'd see to it that happened. Is it beginning to sound wiser to you now?"

Brognola cracked a smile. The President didn't want to come right out and say it, but he was making it obvious that he'd figured out Able Team's ploy, and the gamble had paid off. And unless the G-man missed his guess, the Stony Man team had gotten the Man off the political hook as well.

"Mr. President," Brognola said, "I think that under those circumstances, the plan has considerably more merit."

"Yes, I thought you would. So get somebody to take over at the UN. As soon as that's done, you can relieve Able Team of the assignment." He paused. "And you can tell Lyons and his buddies that I didn't fall off the turnip truck yesterday. I know what they did. Well, their little scheme paid off. They're free to go after the Colombian connection."

"Yes, sir."

"Oh . . . and Hal," the Man said as if in passing.

"Yes, sir?"

"Tell them one other thing for me, will you?"

"Certainly, sir."

"Tell them that if they ever try anything like this again, I'll have *all* your asses on my barbecue grill."

Brognola started to say "Yes, sir" again, but the line had gone dead.

CHARLIE MOTT PULLED the visor of his California *A*'s baseball cap lower against the sun. His tired eyes flickered to the instrument panel, noted the altitude, then returned to the blue morning sky. Settling back into the pilot's seat, his mind wandered briefly to the black silk teddy and matching high heels his girlfriend had just slipped into when the beeper on his belt went off.

Mott forced his thoughts back to the present. "Keep your mind on business, you old fool," he muttered. "You've got other things to worry about right now. Problems that are more important than wondering how a man your age is going to hold on to a twenty-year-old beauty queen."

Blancanales's voice broke into his thoughts from the seat directly behind him. "You say something, Charlie?"

"Just thinking out loud." Mott heard Gadgets Schwarz chuckle.

"You wouldn't be thinking about that little Miss Oregon or whoever it is you been seeing, would you?" Schwarz asked.

Mott grinned. *"Utah,"* he corrected. "Miss Utah. And no, you jealous bastard, my mind never wavers from the mission at hand. Even when it doesn't amount to anything more than chauffeuring around a couple of over-the-hill ground grunts—" he paused, glanced at Carl Lyons in the seat next to him, then added "—and a has-been flatfoot."

He checked the instrument panel again, then slowly pulled back on the control. The plane began its descent into Miami.

A buzz sounded behind Mott and a moment later he heard Schwarz open the case and answer the cellular phone he'd carried on board. "Go ahead, Stony."

Barbara Price's voice came over the speakerphone. "It's a ten-five from Turrin. He's in Key West. Tell Mott to change course. I'll brief you on the way."

Mott lifted the microphone from the instrument panel, contacted the tower and the Cessna began to climb again.

"Leo got next to an old Mafia buddy early this morning," Price went on. "The Family's been keeping tabs on this thing from the start."

"The Mafia's intel network is better than ours half the time," Schwarz commented.

"It almost seems that way," Price agreed. "But keep in mind, their interest is purely financial. They don't care what dope goes where, as long as it doesn't cut into their own territory. And while they've got a firm foothold now in a lot of the former Soviet countries, Stensvik's kept them out of North Haakovia.''

"He's got the death penalty for possession,'' Lyons cut in.

"That's right,'' Price agreed. "But Castro pulls that one every once in a while himself. And we all know Uncle Fidel's hands have been white with dust for years. Anyway, Turrin's buddies are convinced that the cocaine runs the usual route into Medellín, then is shipped aboard several private freighters to Havana. Cuba acts as a refueling stopover before it goes on to the Baltic. What happens to it then is anybody's guess.''

"Striker will find out,'' Blancanales said.

"Affirmative. Let's hope it's soon. I think their assumption about Cuba is sound, and it fits in with Kurtzman's original course projection for the submarine.''

"So what about the sub?'' Lyons asked. "It have anything to do with us going to Key West?''

"Affirmative, Ironman, it's...'' Price's voice trailed off as her intercom buzzed. "Just a second.'' She murmured softly in the background. "Yes, Aaron, I was just about to tell them.'' Price returned to the line. "The sub has changed course. It's heading toward Key West. Forget about the Colombians for the moment, and if it surfaces there, find out what they've got.''

Lyons turned in his seat to speak directly into the speakerphone. "I've got a hunch the two deals are connected. Permission to board and search?''

"As long as it's in U.S. waters, I don't see any problem," Price said.

The big ex-LAPD detective blew air through his nostrils, and Mott suppressed a smile. When he'd been a police officer, Lyons had never liked the loopholes certain rules and regulations allowed for, and he hadn't changed much since joining Able Team. "What if it changes course again," Lyons said, "leaves U.S. territory?"

"Hal's been on the phone with the President again. Because of the sensitivity of all this, and what you guys did to get where you are right now, the Man's insisted on being informed every step of the way. He says stay within jurisdiction. Don't leave U.S. territory."

Lyons shook his head in disgust. "Even if that means losing them?"

"Even if that means losing them. The President says he's got enough international incidents to deal with for the moment, thank you."

Mott checked the instrument panel and started his descent again. A few minutes later, the wheels hit the landing strip on the southernmost island in the Florida Keys.

The Stony Man pilot killed the engines and followed Lyons, Schwarz and Blancanales down from the cockpit. Leo Turrin stood to the side of the strip in front of a black Lincoln Mark IV. The undercover man looked every bit the part of the mafioso he posed as, with his dark features, blown-dry hair, off-white silk suit and open collar.

Lyons didn't waste any time. "Has Kurtzman projected an ETA for the sub yet?"

Turrin flashed the smile that had gotten him through more locked Mafia doors than any other clandestine agent in America. "Hour, maybe an hour and a half. We've got just enough time to get set up."

"Where's the most likely place for it to surface, Leo?"

Turrin indicated the Lincoln with a wave of his hand. "I could tell you, Ironman," he said, opening the door, "but it would be so much more fun to just show you."

9

On the map of the city, Helsinki's city hall didn't appear to be far from the safehouse where Phoenix Force had just neutralized another cell of Dag Vaino's terrorists. But time was running out. They had to move if they were to prevent an assassination.

McCarter braced himself against the dashboard as Gary Manning careered the station wagon around the corner onto Norra Esplanaden. His heart pounded like a kettledrum against his chest and seemed to shoot more adrenaline than blood through his veins and arteries. He jerked the magazine from the Sterling L-2 submachine gun strapped over his shoulder as the car swerved to miss an oncoming vehicle.

McCarter glanced up. Helsinki's Market Square appeared three blocks ahead. The dank odor of the city's South Harbor invaded the Briton's nostrils. He caught a flash of rainbow color as they passed flower stalls and carts bearing mountains of fruit.

The subgun over his right shoulder was hidden from view by a dirty gray overcoat he had liberated from one of the dead terrorists at the safehouse. McCarter checked the magazine, then slammed it back into the weapon. He positioned the awkward side-feeding mag behind his back, pulled the car's visor down in front of him, angled the mirror and looked into it.

McCarter scowled at his reflection. The magazine extended past his back, forcing the coat out sharply on his left side. The Sterling, while one of the most dependable, abuse-resistent and accurate weapons of its type ever invented, hadn't been designed for concealment.

The Briton knew he'd have to keep his left arm down over the hump to keep from being spotted by the police once he reached the site, a bothersome detail during an interval when his mind would be better occupied on the upcoming battle.

McCarter's fingers traced lightly over the four clearance ribs on the bolt as Manning continued to milk the last drop of power out of the station wagon. Then Katz broke the silence, voicing the concerns of the rest of the team.

"We'll be limited on firepower," the Israeli leader said. "We can take nothing that can't be hidden under our coats. So grab as many extra side arms and all the ammo you think you can carry and still move."

McCarter drew the Browning Hi-Power from his hip holster. Cocked and locked. He'd brought an identical backup Browning with him to Finland, and the second 14-shot 9 mm pistol rode jammed against his ribs in his waistband. A "six-pack" of extra clips rode on his belt, and he'd filled the pockets of the trench coat with enough loose rounds to sink a ship.

The former SAS officer dropped the mag from the second Browning, then returned it to his belt. The Hi-

Powers and Sterling used interchangeable ammunitions, which was a good thing.

He had a feeling a lot of ammo was about to be used up.

Tilting the visor slightly, McCarter looked into the back seat and saw Calvin James adding a second Beretta to his arsenal. The rest of the members of Phoenix Force had done the same.

Manning slowed the station wagon as they reached the presidential palace, then dropped it to a crawl as they drew even with the crowd outside city hall. Ahead, on the other side of the intersecting street, he saw the tourist information office.

The Briton studied the congregation in front of the building and breathed a sigh of relief. The assembly at the front steps wasn't as large as it could have been. Maybe four to five hundred people had come out in the cold to hear Risto Kalle speak. They stood along the sidewalk in front of city hall, listening to the frosty-haired figure behind the podium at the top of the steps.

Risto Kalle, the Finnish "hawk" in favor of returning both North and South Haakovia to Finland, shouted passionately into the microphone.

The crowd cheered its approval.

"Stop and let us out," Katz ordered Manning, "then find a place to park. Someplace out of the way. We don't know what will happen, but remember—the Finns don't know we're the good guys. When, and if, it hits the fan, we'll have targets on our foreheads just like Vaino and his men."

"That's for sure," Manning said as he pulled to a stop along the curb. "If things get bad, where do we regroup?"

Katz paused. He glanced to the roof of the station wagon and frowned. Then, looking back down, he said, "Stay away from the car. We'll need it later, so I don't want it fingered. Better meet somewhere a long way from here. The national opera theater is on Bulevardi. Know it?"

"Been awhile since Cal and I hit the Helsinki opera," Encizo said, grinning, "but we'll find it."

Katz, James, Encizo and McCarter exited the van and stopped at the edge of the crowd as Manning drove away. "We'll circle the perimeter and cut a swath right through the middle," Katz whispered. "Rafael, go left. James, right. McCarter, you and I will head straight through the crowd. Look for anything suspicious, and we'll meet back here in—" he glanced at his wrist "—ten"

The Stony Man warriors nodded and took off.

McCarter held his left arm out from his side, doing his best to camouflage the protruding subgun magazine. The listeners seemed intent on Kalle's fervent words, and no one seemed to notice as The Phoenix Force veteran threaded his way through the crowd.

The Briton's eyes flickered from face to face. He had fought terrorists for more years than he cared to remember, first as a commando leader with the British Special Air Service, then as a member of one of Stony Man Farm's two elite counterterrorist teams.

He knew exactly the profile he was looking for.

David McCarter gently shoved his way from person to person, scanning each man and woman for signs of tension. Shifting eyes, a facial tic, a trembling hand. Anything that would lead one to believe that the person demonstrating the trait had more on his or her mind than simply Risto Kalle's inflammatory speech.

The Phoenix Force warrior had found no such evidence by the time he reached the front edge of the crowd, and he turned around and began making his way back toward the street. Through breaks in the huddled pack he caught glimpses of Katz doing the same a few feet away. Once or twice he spotted James just outside the ring of listeners.

By the time he got back to the street, Manning had returned.

"Anything?" the big Canadian asked.

McCarter shook his head. "But I didn't really expect to find anything. Vaino and his men are as professional as they come. And on such short notice, there's no way to adequately—"

The loud crack of a rifle round rang out suddenly, cutting him off. Both men bolted to the steps.

Kalle's mouth fell open in shock.

Slowly, as if in slow-motion instant replay, a small round hole appeared in the middle of Kalle's forehead. Then the film seemed to speed up as a jet of crimson shot suddenly from the hole and washed down like a waterfall over the Finn's eyes and nose. Then he dropped to the ground.

The crowd, for a moment as shocked as Kalle, remained silent. A second later they came to their senses and the screams began.

McCarter turned toward the direction from which the shot had come—the tourist information office. His fingers found the grip of the Sterling beneath his coat as his eyes started on the roof, moving methodically down the face of the building.

Two floors from the top, a rifle barrel jerked back inside a window.

The Briton hadn't seen the sniper's face, but he knew who had fired the shot.

Dag Vaino.

McCarter was moving toward the building when he heard tires shriek to a halt behind him. His training and instinct demanded that he turn around.

He did. And none too soon.

Half a dozen men wearing black ski masks and matching coveralls leaped from a white panel truck. Danish Hoveas and Madsen M-50s appeared in the masked men's gloved hands. The submachine guns bucked and jerked as the terrorists fired a steady stream of rounds into the crowd.

More screams erupted within the mass as several people fell under the bloody assault.

McCarter dropped to one knee. He swung the Sterling from under his coat. Gripping the fore end with his left hand, he squeezed the trigger and sent a burst into the chest of the closest terrorist.

A second panel truck skidded to a halt twenty feet to the rear of the first and disgorged another hit team.

Brass casings rained through the air as they opened up with their weapons.

McCarter swung the Sterling their way, cutting a figure eight through the group and downing two more men. To his left he saw a woman who'd been watching Kalle from the rear of the crowd. She ripped open her coat, then leaned forward into the baby carriage in front of her and jerked a blanket from around a Sako-Valmet AB.

McCarter turned the Sterling her way. As his finger moved the trigger back, he caught a glimmer of steel from under the open overcoat. His finger beat a hasty retreat toward the front of the trigger guard as her badge came into focus.

The woman twisted toward the vans and opened fire on the terrorists.

Several more undercover cops threw off their overcoats to reveal badges. They entered the thunderstorm with Suomi Model 44 submachine guns and Lahti M-35 pistols blazing. A dozen uniformed cops and an equal number of Finnish soldiers appeared as if from nowhere to join the melee.

McCarter was suddenly aware of James standing at his side. The black warrior dropped to his knees to fire, Berettas jumping in both hands.

Two more of Vaino's backup men bit the dirt. A third turned a full three-sixty, his hands clutching a wounded knee.

The sharp odor of burned cordite filled McCarter's nostrils as he sent a short burst into the limping man's chest, taking the masked terrorist out of the action.

The roar of another vehicle sounded through a break in the bedlam. McCarter looked up to see a third truck speeding toward the crowd from the opposite direction. Several masked men hung from the running boards, while others leaned from the windows brandishing subguns.

But the real threat was mounted on top of the truck—a Chinese Type 75-1 machine gun.

The Briton turned, firing at the man behind the weapon. The panel truck swerved, ruining his aim, and the burst sailed high.

The barrel of the 75-1 swung toward McCarter, who dived to his right, rolling as a volley of 14.5 × 114 mm rounds blasted into the sidewalk where he'd knelt. Dust flew through the air, falling like snow onto his trench coat, and razor-edged chips of concrete pelted his face and neck. McCarter kept rolling, the masked machine gunner's assault following his movement, always less than a roll behind.

A sharp series of cracks sounded suddenly above McCarter's head, and the machine gun stopped firing abruptly.

The Briton rolled to a halt. He saw Katz standing several yards away, the little Steyr still barking in the Israeli's hand. The former SAS officer looked back to the panel truck.

The machine gunner hung from the side of the roof by his straps, his head bobbing limply in time to Katz's rounds.

McCarter slammed a fresh mag into the side of the Sterling. In the corner of his eye he saw a uniformed cop turn toward him. Mistaking him for a terrorist, the cop raised his Lahti.

The Briton dropped to the earth a split second before the officer's pistol bucked in his hand. The shot sailed high.

As the officer aimed again, a masked man stepped up behind him and fired almost point-blank into the back of the cop's head, neutralizing the threat for McCarter. The officer went down.

McCarter thanked the terrorist with a volley of parabellums. As the man sprawled over the dead cop, the Phoneix Force warrior turned to fire again, this time into the center of a trio of men who had leaped from the third truck. Two more masked men went down. The third took a short burst in the side as he scrambled to the top of the panel truck, trying desperately to reach the machine gun.

The Sterling ran dry.

Four terrorists ran for cover as McCarter dropped the subgun to the end of the sling and ripped a Browning from his belt. He watched Katz take out the men with the Steyr as he brought the pistol up.

Only one of Vaino's men remained as McCarter swung the Hi-Power on the second panel truck, raised it to eye-level and lined up the sights. But before he could fire, Encizo appeared in his peripheral vision. The little Cuban's Beretta spit twice.

As suddenly as the terrorists had appeared, their threat had been erased. But in their place, a new threat suddenly reared its head. Unaware of who they were, the Finnish cops turned toward the men of Phoenix Force.

Katz's voice screamed over the confusion. His order was straight, simple, direct—"Scatter!"

His men did as they were told.

McCarter caught glimpses of James and Encizo taking off in opposite directions as he sprinted across the street toward Market Square. A flurry of rounds from the police officers' weapons skidded across the pavement to his sides. One of the rounds hit the street just behind him, skimmed across the pavement and tore the heel from his black leather paratrooper boot.

The Briton went sprawling face-first into a strawberry cart. The police quit firing while the confused vendor dived away from the action. As McCarter rolled under the cart his leg hit the wheel, overturning it, and an avalanche of strawberries slid down over his head and shoulders. He sprang back to his feet, sprinting on toward the waters of South Harbor.

Another volley of rounds urged him on as the Briton reached the three-foot wall surrounding the harbor. He felt a sizzling sensation as a bullet tore through his pant leg, scorching across his skin. He took three final steps, his right foot landing on top of the wall.

Then David McCarter was airborne. A moment later he was plummeting into the icy cold waters of Helsinki's South Harbor.

WHENEVER SHE SAT alone behind the massive oak desk in the presidential office, Janyte Varkaus couldn't help feeling out of place. The padded, oversize leather chair her husband had ordered custom-built was a replica of one he'd seen years ago at the White House.

It was tall, as he had been, and barely let her feet brush the ground.

The vast room itself, on the third floor of the ancient Finnish castle, had been fashioned to his specifications by tearing down the existing walls within six smaller sleeping areas. Shaped in an oval, it, too, reflected her husband's visit to Washington, D.C. Edvaard had overseen the remodeling himself, and made sure the workmen followed to the letter the detailed plans he had drawn out. The walls were a nonreflective, subdued off-white that the late South Haakovian president had known would be perfect for televised interviews. Except for the seal of Haakovia, the carpet was an exact replica of that in the office of the President of the United States.

Janyte's mind drifted back to her husband during those early days of both his presidency and their marriage. It had been a busy time, and Edvaard had exuded a vibrancy like no man she had ever known before. He had been so driven, so dedicated to throwing off the yoke of Communist repression, so certain that someday Haakovia would become the leading economic and political force in the Baltics.

"So confident. So sure of himself," Janyte whispered. She heard the voice echo softly off the walls of the empty room. "Was that what attracted me to him?"

Janyte rotated the mammoth chair and faced the Haakovian flag on the pole behind the desk. Her eyes stared dully at the fabric. Had she ever really loved Edvaard? Or had what she believed to be love been no more than the infatuation of a young girl for an older, powerful man?

Janyte sighed. She didn't know. Perhaps she never would. But of one thing she was certain. Somewhere along the line, whatever her feelings were, they had vanished as she gradually lost more and more respect for her husband. She had seen firsthand the methods Edvaard used to bring about his goal. Blackmail had been only one of his tricks, and however right, just and moral it might have been to turn Haakovia into a democracy, the means Edvaard Varkaus had used to reach that end never seemed justified.

Janyte's mind flashed briefly to Quenby Knudsen, and for a moment the shame she'd felt upon leaving the office of the homosexual minister of the interior returned. Then the shame turned to anger as she realized even *that* had been Edvaard's fault.

She scowled at the flag. Her husband had left her in a position in which she didn't want to be. His death had forced her to use the same seedy, deceitful means he had used to keep South Haakovia from crumbling. It was his fault, and that knowledge did nothing to make her memory of Edvaard a fond one.

Janyte pictured Edvaard now, at the funeral parlor being prepared for the services that would take place in the castle chapel the next day. She tried to conjure some amount of grief, some form of sorrow. To a degree she was successful.

But no more so than if the funeral was for some distant acquaintance.

The phone behind her buzzed suddenly and she jumped in her seat. She twirled around and lifted the receiver to her ear. "Yes?"

"Colonel Pollock is here," her secretary said.

"Send him in."

The new president of South Haakovia drew in a deep breath, trying to calm her nerves. She was in no mood for decisions today. She didn't even feel up to deciding what dress to wear, let alone leading her country into the war that appeared inevitable.

As the door opened, Janyte stood quickly, hurrying around the desk to stand in front of it.

Colonel Rance Pollock walked into her office.

Janyte studied the man as he approached her. Pollock wore a clean, carefully pressed U.S. army uniform. The front of his shirt was bare of medals, but Janyte couldn't help thinking that might be because there were just too many to fit a chest even as broad as his. Her eyes moved up to his face. Pollock's jaw was set firm. His own eyes seemed to bore holes through hers, similar to the way Edvaard's had done when her husband had been in one of his frequent rages. But Pollock's eyes reflected no rage, no anger. The probing orbs set within the colonel's dark, chiseled features displayed a quiet seriousness, a certainty of himself, a vibrancy. A dedication to...

Cause, Janyte almost said out loud. Like Edvaard.

"Good morning, Madam President," Bolan said.

"Please, Colonel Pollock. Sit down."

"Thank you."

Janyte smoothed her skirt under her as she settled into the love seat across from Bolan. Suddenly she was conscious of her makeup, her hair, the tiny, almost invisible scar on her chin where she had fallen against the side of her swing set as a girl. "You wished to see me immediately, Colonel?"

"Yes."

Pollock continued to stare at her. Janyte fought the urge to look away, for there was something in those eyes that both aroused and frightened her. It had nothing to do with the immense strength, both physical and moral, that she read in his face. For along with the strength, the eyes told her that Pollock was a loyal soldier, a man of his word. A man who would never use his power for evil, or even use evil means to accomplish righteous goals as Edvaard had done.

Then what was it that frightened her? Janyte wondered. Could it be that, unless she missed her guess, she saw a flicker of interest in Pollock's eyes, as well?

"I am sorry, Colonel Pollock. My mind is preoccupied today."

"That's understandable."

"Would you mind repeating what you just said?"

"I said we have a problem with General Markus."

The president listened as he explained about the long-range night lens that had never arrived at the airport.

"Colonel Pollock," she said when he'd finished, "isn't it possible that the orders were legitimately confused?"

Bolan shrugged. "Anything's possible, Madam President. But in view of this mission's sensitivity, Markus should have made sure the lens got to me, even if that meant he had to hand deliver it personally." He shook his head. "No ma'am, this was no accident. Markus did it on purpose. And it's symptomatic of a larger problem."

"And what is that?"

"Simply put, Markus doesn't like me. That's to be expected. Understandable, considering that I showed up suddenly and stole part of his show. But it could go even deeper than that. It's not unheard of, but it's rare that a general would risk a mission as important as mine was for personal revenge." He paused. "Tell me, Madam President. How well do you know Markus?"

Janyte shrugged. "Not well. But he and my husband were close. He was one of the few men Edvaard trusted."

"I know what I'm about to say isn't a comfortable subject with you," he said, "but I need to know. Have you checked to see if your husband had anything on him in his files?"

"Yes. There is a file, but it is empty."

"That could mean any of a number of things. Did President Varkaus have files on everyone, even if he'd gathered no evidence yet? Are there other empty files?"

"No. Only the general's."

Bolan nodded. "Then it doesn't sound like his standard M.O. My guess is he wouldn't bother to start a file until he had something to put in it. Which leads me to believe there *was* something there at one time. That means he cleaned it out himself for one reason or another or—"

"Or Markus gained access and destroyed the evidence himself."

"Exactly."

Janyte turned and looked at the wall. Everything seemed to be closing in at once. She wished she had never met Edvaard Varkus, never come to Haakovia, never...

"I don't have enough evidence to convict him of treason," Bolan went on. "I don't even have enough to be sure myself. But my gut instinct tells me there's a good chance Markus is dirty."

"What do we do?"

"Take the bull by the horns. Under the circumstances, we don't have time for anything else. If he's dirty, replacing him won't be easy. And the sooner we get started the better."

Janyte sat quietly, trying to concentrate on what the colonel had said. But it was becoming increasingly difficult to keep her mind from drifting. The unbelievable pressures that accompanied the presidency, combined with her attraction for the American, made her want to jump up and run from the room.

"I am sorry, Colonel Pollock," she said. "This is all...so confusing. Please, sum up the situation for me as best you can."

Janyte watched Pollock study her. He knew how she felt, about both her job and him. She could tell he sensed it. He took his time answering, and she knew he was choosing his words carefully. That, too, reminded her of Edvaard, for the late president of South Haakovia had been a master politican. Edvaard's words had often been distorted, and sometimes baldfaced lies. But he'd been an artist at saying the right things to the right people at the right times.

But when Pollock finally spoke, he didn't sound like Edvaard. He didn't sound like a politician at all, and Janyte Varkaus suddenly realized that while Pollock might share many strengths with her late husband, he harbored none of Edvaard Varkaus's gray-area morality. Rance Pollock was honest, straightforward and to the point.

A different breed altogether from her husband.

"General Markus is either jealous of me, or incompetent," Pollock said bluntly. "Or he's a traitor."

Janyte sat quietly for several moments. "Need we confront him. Should I call him in?"

Bolan nodded. "I took the liberty of doing that myself, Madam President." He glanced to his watch. "He should be outside now."

Janyte nodded. As if on cue, the phone buzzed, and she punched the speakerphone.

"Madam President," the secretary said over the intercom, "General Markus is here and asks when you will be ready for him." Markus's deep, gravelly voice rumbled incoherently in the background. "He, uh, says he is extremely busy," the secretary stammered, "and wonders if he should come back later."

Janyte glanced at the Executioner. Bolan shook his head.

"Send him in."

A moment later, Genrral Markus swaggered into the office, his pencil mustache tightening slightly when he saw Bolan seated across from Janyte. Markus wore the OD green uniform of the South Haakovian army, but had added his own touches. The kepi atop his head made him look like he'd just stepped out of a French foreign legion movie. White web gear circled his waist, and a gold-plated Grizzly .45 Winchester Magnum MKI protruded from the top of his holster. Beneath the web belt, the general had tied a royal blue cummerbund.

The parachute brevet on Markus's right breast puffed out in importance as he strode toward the sofas. Ignoring Bolan, he addressed Janyte. "You wish to see me, Madam President?"

"Please, sit down, General Markus." She indicated the sofa next to Bolan.

The Executioner watched the haughty little officer smooth the crease in his trousers as he sat. He studied the man out of the corner of his eye. He hadn't lied to Janyte Varkaus—it was too early to be certain that Markus was dirty. But even if the general was simply jealous, lazy or incompetent, the problem had to be nipped in the bud before it became more serious.

And with the situation with North Haakovia ready to boil over at any moment, there was no time for anything but laying things on the line and trying to read the general's reactions.

Janyte looked across the room to the two men. "Colonel Pollock, please take over."

Bolan turned to face Markus. "I'll be brief. We've had communication problems so far, and your failure to provide the long-range camera lens almost blew the mission to Sturegorsk."

Markus refused to look at the Executioner. "Madam President, *you* have my deepest apologies. The equipment this man requested was incorrectly routed to the wrong landing field. By the time the mistake was discovered, Colonel Pollock had already left." Markus cleared his throat. "The NCO responsible for the mistake had already been disciplined." He turned to Bolan for the first time, but continued to speak as if the Executioner were not in the room. "Had Colonel Pollock had the patience to wait a few more minutes, the lens would have been delivered to him." Markus's thin mustache curled up in an arrogant smile.

Bolan fought the temptation to reach over, grab Markus by the neck and shake some humility into him. What had happened might really have been an honest mistake, but even if it was, the Executioner could see that the general was a master of bureaucratic gibberish. He was the type of officer who passed the blame down, around, right or left, forward or back, wherever it would go without rebounding on him. Markus had probably built his career around never being able to be pinned down.

"Let's cut through the crap, General," Bolan growled. "This was a sensitive mission, and the responsibility for this foul-up rests firmly on our epaulets. Whatever happened, I hold *you* responsible."

Blood flooded to Markus's face as his thin chest seemingly swelled to twice its size. The skin of his face stretched tight, threatening to burst like an overinflated balloon. "Who are you to speak to me like this?" he demanded, vaulting to his feet. He stared down at the Executioner, his eyes glowing embers of hatred. "If you were under my command, I would have you court-martialed!"

Bolan looked up at him. "But I'm not under your command. And I want to make one thing perfectly clear. This is your free one, Markus. Do something like this again, and I'll deal with you myself."

Frustration covered the general's face for a moment, then the anger and hatred returned. "I will deal with *you* myself," he shouted and drew back a fist.

The Executioner reached up as the fist flew toward his face. He caught it in the palm of his hand, closed his fingers around the knuckles and twisted Markus's wrist.

The general flopped back to a sitting position on the couch.

Janyte leaned forward. "Tread lightly, General Markus. Perform your duties and make certain that we have no more problems like this." She straightened. "You are dismissed."

Markus opened his mouth to speak. He closed it just as quickly, stood, straightened his uniform and hurried from the room.

Janyte smiled at Bolan as soon as the general had gone. "That was not easy for me."

"I know. But you did it well."

"I hope I can trust you, Colonel Pollock..." she said.

"You can."

"Because in essence, you are helping me run South Haakovia." When the Executioner didn't answer, she said, "The question now is, can we trust General Markus?"

Bolan nodded. "So long as he's in sight." He paused, looking at the door through which Markus had disappeared, again wondering if the problem with the long-range lens had been a mistake or a deliberate act of sabotage.

He still didn't know. But he *did* know one thing.

He had humiliated Gustaf Markus when he caught the punch and dropped him back to the couch like a child. And when a proud man like Markus lost respect in the eyes of a beautiful woman, he might go to any length to get it back.

Bolan knew it would serve him well not to turn his back on the man.

"What do we do now?" Janyte asked.

Bolan shrugged and stood. "Get ready for a funeral," he replied. "And a war."

THE SUN HAD GONE DOWN and the temperature fallen twenty degrees as Rafael Encizo walked down Bulevardi toward the national opera theater. He'd been lucky escaping the police outside city hall, drawing only meager pursuit for the first few minutes.

But that hadn't put the little Cuban's mind at ease. There had been a lot of cops at Risto Kalle's speech, and if they hadn't chased him, that meant they'd gone after the other four members of Phoenix Force.

Encizo strolled on, trying to look like a tourist and making a point of gazing through the closed shop windows at the displays of glassware, wooden toys and metal jewelry for which Helsinki was famous. The odor of melting wax filled his head as he passed a candle factory, and then the wax smell turned to lacquer as he neared a handmade furniture mill.

He pulled the collar of his ski parka around his throat as he walked on. He had hidden the filthy trench coat and his weapons in an alley earlier in the afternoon, ducked into the Bellevue restaurant on Rahapajankatu Street, walked directly to the coatroom and demanded the first wrap he saw from the checkout girl. She hadn't asked to see his ticket, and he'd left the restaurant with both the parka and a stocking cap that effectively altered his appearance from what it had been outside city hall. The coat was at least two sizes too large, but Encizo wasn't complaining. The guns under the goose-down lining filled it out perfectly.

Encizo stopped at a bench outside the ornately decorated theater building. Where were Katz and the rest of the team? He had escaped easily, so easily that he had purposely taken a circuitous route around the city, boarding and exiting buses until he was certain he hadn't been followed.

He shouldn't have been the first of the team to arrive at the opera house.

Katz suddenly appeared in front of him. The Phoenix Force leader frowned down at him. ''None of the others are here?''

Encizo stood and shook his head.

The Israeli nodded, but the frown stayed in place. He glanced quickly up and down the street. ''We can't all congregate here in public,'' he said. ''The cops will still be looking for us.'' His eyes stopped suddenly and his face relaxed.

Encizo followed Katz's gaze.

The Phoenix Force leader turned back. "The Grand Hotel is just up the street. I'll go get a room. Wait here and send everyone there as soon as they arrive. I'll register as Samuel Wilenzick of Haifa."

Encizo sat back down on the bench and Katz hurried away.

Several minutes later, he heard a voice.

"Got a light, buddy?"

Encizo looked up to see Gary Manning stick a rumpled cigarette between his lips. A tiny smile tugged at the corners of the big Canadian's face.

The Cuban grinned back. The cigarette was more than just a reason to approach him in front of any eyes that might be watching—it was an inside joke. Neither he nor Manning smoked, and their negative feelings about those who did bordered on extremism.

"You have any trouble?" Encizo asked.

Manning shook his head. "Not after everybody quit shooting at me."

"Katz has gone to get a hotel room. Seen any of the others?"

"Just the bottoms of their boots as they left."

Encizo nodded toward the hotel. "The Grand, down the street. There's a Mr. Wilenzick waiting there for you."

"Know which room?"

Encizo looked down at the sidewalk and shook his head. "You think I can do all your work for you?"

Manning shrugged. "Wish somebody would." He stuck the cigarette into his pocket before walking away.

Calvin James arrived a few minutes later. Two small holes ran through the bottom of his sweatshirt, the edges of both browned from heat.

"It hit you?" Encizo asked.

"Just a nick. I got worse as a kid from my old man."

"Grand Hotel. Sam Wilenzick," Encizo told him, and James walked away.

Encizo continued to wait, his heart again filling with apprehension. The last he had seen of David McCarter, the former SAS officer had been under heavy fire and headed toward the market area. And while the little Cuban might not know Helsinki like the back of his hand, he knew what lay past the carts and vendors.

The harbor. A dead end.

The opera ended and men and women in formal dress exited the theater, chattering excitedly.

The fear in his chest continued to build.

It was nearly midnight when the little Cuban finally stood up. He walked slowly, glancing over his shoulder every few steps, silently praying he'd see David McCarter walking up to the theater.

Rafael Encizo picked up his pace, walking faster.

But if McCarter was coming, he'd have been here by now. That could mean only one of two things.

Suddenly, Encizo started to run toward the Grand Hotel. McCarter had been captured or he was dead.

It was time to regroup.

And to go find out which.

EPILOGUE

The cold stone walls and staircase seemed appropriate for the atmosphere of threat that pervaded Larsborg Castle.

Mack Bolan descended the steps outside Janyte Varkaus's office. Reaching the floor below, he turned the corner and started down the hall toward the chapel.

Uniformed men, both American Special Forces and what was trying to pass for the South Haakovian equivalent, saluted as he passed.

The Executioner nodded back.

He stopped outside the chapel door, then glanced inside. Several men wearing green berets were scanning the pews, walls and dais with metal detectors. Others swept the room for electronic-surveillance devices, as still more Special Forces soldiers stood guard at the windows.

South Haakovia had no special reason to believe Franzen Stensvik had anything planned for the funeral. On the other hand, there had been no special reason to believe he would assassinate Edvaard Varkaus during the television interview.

Bolan's eyes fell on the space in front of the pulpit where the casket would rest during the next morning's service. For the time being the warrior had ordered that Edvaard Varkaus's body be kept under guard at the funeral home where the late South Haakovian president had been embalmed. The mixed contingent of Americans and South Haakovians would watch over the remains until secretly transferring them sometime during the night.

The Executioner heard a bark and turned around. A South Haakovian army K-9 bomb squad entered the chapel. Bolan stepped aside, and the German Shepherd led his master up the aisle, the dog's snout an inch off the ground.

Continuing down the hall, Bolan came to the temporary security-communications room he had set up. Four soldiers stood guard outside the door. They stood aside while the Executioner fished his key-card out of his shirt pocket and inserted it into the slot. The door buzzed open.

Bolan stepped inside. The handful of S.H. army computer experts seated around the room looked up to meet his gaze. He knew none of the men and women personally, and with even the South Haakovian military commander's allegiance in question, he intended to take no chances. "Take five," he said.

"Take what?"

"A break."

"All of us?"

"All of you."

Their faces covered with curiosity, the computer operators filed out of the room.

Bolan shut and locked the door behind them. He lifted the telephone and dialed Stony Man Farm, double-checking the scrambling device on his end.

Thirty seconds later, he had Barbara Price on the phone. "Your scrambler on?" he asked.

"That's affirmative."

"Update me," the Executioner requested.

"Katz is on the other line right now. Phoenix Force is lying low at a hotel in Helsinki. They got there too late to save Kalle, and they've been a step behind Vaino all the way." She paused, and Bolan heard her take a deep breath. "And McCarter's missing."

"Do they have any idea where he is?"

"Negative. Somewhere in Helsinki. They shot it out with a large force of terrorists after Vaino took out Kalle. Then the cops turned on them and they had to split up. Rafael saw McCarter head toward the harbor, but he never showed up at the rendezvous."

Bolan paused. With his SAS training, David McCarter was as good as they came. If anybody could still be alive under those conditions, it would be him.

"Okay, tell Katz to start looking. That's his first priority...but he'll know that. How about Able Team? They find out anything about the cartel connection yet?"

"Negative. They've gotten sidetracked for the moment. Bear's got the submarine's course charted for Key West. Able Team is there now with Turrin, waiting for the sub to surface."

"Where's Hal?"

"He's at the White House with the Man. They told me to patch you through if you touched base."

"I'll wait."

The Executioner drummed his fingers against the top of the console as he waited. Finally he heard the President's voice.

"What's the outlook, Striker?" the Man asked.

Bolan thought back to the preparations he had seen under way at Lenin naval base in North Haakovia. "Everything points toward war, Mr. President."

There was a long pause at the other end, and as he listened to the line crackle and snap, the Executioner thought of the other Americans risking their lives that Haakovia might be free.

McCarter could already be dead. Phoenix Force was under fire from both Dag Vaino's terrorists and the Finnish police, and Able Team was about to take on a nuclear submarine.

For the moment the men from Stony Man Farm were safe. But the seconds were ticking away.

The President cleared his throat. "Can you guess at the time frame? Have you any idea *when* Stensvik will begin?"

"Any second, Mr. President," he said. "Any second."

* * * * *

*The heart-stopping action continues
in the second book of The Freedom Trilogy:
#175, Battle Ground, coming in July.*

Communism's death throes bring the
world to the edge of doom in

DON PENDLETON'S

THE EXECUTIONER®

FEATURING

MACK BOLAN®

BATTLE
FORCE

The dynamic conclusion to the FREEDOM TRILOGY finds Mack
Bolan, Able Team and Phoenix Force battling to avert World
War III. From the war-torn states of Eastern Europe to the urban
hellgrounds of Los Angeles, Bolan's army fights to head off a
nightmare of chemical warfare.

Omega Force is caught dead center in a brutal Middle East war
in the next episode of

OMEGA

by PATRICK F. ROGERS

In Book 2: **ZERO HOUR,** the Omega Force is dispatched on a
search-and-destroy mission to eliminate enemies of the U.S.
seeking revenge for Iraq's defeat in the Gulf—enemies who will
use any means necessary to trigger a full-scale war.

With capabilities unmatched by any other paramilitary organi-
zation in the world, Omega Force is a special ready-reaction anti-
terrorist strike force composed of the best commandos and
equipment the military has to offer.